£3.50

171331

D0269116

KING'

OXFORD BOOKWORMS LIBRARY

Crime & Mystery

King's Ransom

Stage 5 (1800 headwords)

Series Editor: Jennifer Bassett
Founder Editor: Tricia Hedge
Activities Editors: Jennifer Bassett and Alison Baxter

ED McBAIN

King's Ransom

Retold from the original novel by
Rosalie Kerr

OXFORD UNIVERSITY PRESS

OXFORD

UNIVERSITY PRESS

Great Clarendon Street, Oxford OX2 6DP

Oxford University Press is a department of the University of Oxford.
It furthers the University's objective of excellence in research, scholarship,
and education by publishing worldwide in

Oxford New York

Auckland Cape Town Dar es Salaam Hong Kong Karachi
Kuala Lumpur Madrid Melbourne Mexico City Nairobi
New Delhi Shanghai Taipei Toronto

With offices in

Argentina Austria Brazil Chile Czech Republic France Greece
Guatemala Hungary Italy Japan Poland Portugal Singapore
South Korea Switzerland Thailand Turkey Ukraine Vietnam

OXFORD and OXFORD ENGLISH are registered trade marks of
Oxford University Press in the UK and in certain other countries

ISBN 978 0 19 479230 1

A complete recording of this Bookworms edition of
King's Ransom is available on audio CD ISBN 978 0 19 479208 0

Typeset by Wyvern Typesetting Ltd, Bristol

Printed in Hong Kong

ACKNOWLEDGEMENTS
Illustrated by: Mark Thomas

Word count (main text): 22,670 words

For more information on the Oxford Bookworms Library,
visit www.oup.com/elt/bookworms

CONTENTS

1

'We want your voting stock, Doug'

Outside the window boats sailed up and down the River Harb. In the clear October air, orange and gold leaves screamed their colour against the cold blue sky.

The room was full of cigarette smoke. It hung over the five men like the breath of ghosts. The room was enormous, but it was full now, full of the dirty ash-trays, used glasses and empty bottles left at the end of a long and difficult discussion. The men themselves were as exhausted as the smoky air.

Tired but determined, the men sitting opposite Douglas King hammered out their argument. King listened to them silently.

'We're asking you to think about profit, Doug, that's all,' George Benjamin said. 'Is that a lot to ask?'

'Think of shoes, yes,' Rudy Stone said. 'Don't forget shoes. But think of profit. Granger Shoe is a business, Doug, a business. Profit and loss. The black and the red.'

'And our job,' Benjamin said, 'is to keep Granger in the black. Now take another look at these shoes.'

A thin man, he moved fast and silently to a glass table, which was covered with women's shoes. He picked one up from the pile and gave it to King.

'What woman wants to buy a shoe like this?' he asked.

'Don't misunderstand us,' Stone said quickly. He was a muscular blond man who looked much younger than his forty-five years. 'It's a good shoe, a fine shoe, but we're thinking of profit now.'

1

'The red and the black,' Benjamin repeated. He turned to an older man sitting beside him. 'Am I right, Frank?'

'One hundred per cent,' Frank Blake said, in a thick Southern accent. He blew cigarette smoke at the high ceiling.

'The American housewife,' Benjamin said, 'can't afford this shoe. But even if she *could* afford it, she wouldn't want it. Mrs America, our customer. The stupidest little woman in the world.'

'We've got to excite her, Doug.'

'You're a married man, Doug. What excites Mrs King?'

Pete Cameron, King's assistant, was standing at the bar at the back of the room. He smiled at King, but King did not smile back. He stared at Benjamin.

'Clothes excite a woman!' Stone said.

'Dresses, hats, jackets, bags, *shoes*!' Benjamin said, his voice rising.

'Profit depends on excitement,' Stone said. 'You can't excite a woman with these shoes. There's just no excitement at all in these shoes!'

The room was silent for a moment.

Then Douglas King said, 'What are we selling? Shoes or a good time in bed?'

Frank Blake rose to his feet. 'Doug is making a joke,' he said. 'But it's my money I'm interested in, not jokes. I hold a lot of stock in this company, and I can see now why Granger is almost in the red.'

'Frank is right, Doug,' Benjamin said. 'This is nothing to make jokes about. We have to do something fast to save Granger Shoe.'

'What do you want from me?' King asked softly.

'Now you're asking the right questions,' Benjamin said. 'Give us all another drink, will you, Pete?'

Cameron began mixing the drinks. A tall and handsome man of thirty-five, he moved quickly and watched the others as he worked.

'All right, Doug,' Benjamin said. 'We're the top men in Granger Shoe. I'm sales chief, you're production, and Rudy here is fashion and design. We're all on the board of directors, and we all know what's wrong with the company.'

'What's that?' King asked.

'The Old Man.'

'What does he know about women's tastes? What does he know about *women*?' Stone said. 'But he's president of Granger. Year after year, he's president, because he has enough stock to keep it that way.'

'And the company goes down and down.'

'And my stock is worth less and less each year,' Frank Blake said.

King watched, as Benjamin went quickly to the glass table and picked up a red shoe. 'Look at this!' he said. 'This is what I mean by excitement!'

'Made up from my own design,' Rudy Stone said proudly. 'Take a good look at it, Doug.'

'Women will love it,' Benjamin said. 'What do women know about quality, as long as the shoe looks good?'

King turned the shoe over in his big hands, saying nothing.

'I know what he's thinking,' Stone said. 'He's thinking the Old Man would never let Granger make a shoe like that.'

'But the Old Man won't have anything to say about it. That's why we're here today.'

'Oh, is that why we're here?' King said, smiling. Only Cameron smiled back at him.

'The Old Man's got twenty-five per cent of the voting stock,' Benjamin said.

'The Old Man's got twenty-five per cent,' King said quietly, 'and you, Rudy and Frank have twenty-one per cent between you. Not enough to fight the Old Man and win. What's on your mind?'

'Control,' Stone said.

'Control,' Benjamin repeated. 'We want your voting stock, Doug. You've got thirteen per cent. Come in with us, and we'll have thirty-four per cent. More than enough to get the Old Man out. How about it, Doug? With a shoe like this one we'll take control of the cheap end of the market and kill the competition.'

'George is right,' Blake said. 'I don't care what kind of shoes we sell, as long as we make money.'

'Who will be the new president?' King asked.

There was a short silence. 'We think George Benjamin should be president,' Stone said.

'Well now,' King said dryly. 'That's a surprise.'

'With you as vice-president, of course,' Stone said quickly, 'at a much larger salary than you get now.'

Douglas King rose slowly to his feet. He was tall, with the hard muscle and wide shoulders of a diver. At forty-two years old, his hair was turning grey, but this only added to the strong character which showed in his face and his blue eyes.

'You'll sell a shoe like this, George?' he asked. 'You'll use the Granger name on a cheap shoe?'

'Yes, that's right. It's a good idea, isn't it?'

'Profits will be higher,' Blake said.

'The Old Man may have faults,' King said, 'but he's always made an honest shoe. You want to make garbage.'

'Now wait just a second, Doug—'

'No, *you* wait a second! I like Granger Shoe. I've worked for this company since I was sixteen. I know shoes. Good shoes. *Quality*. I won't put the Granger name on a piece of garbage!' With one quick movement of his strong hands, he tore the shoe to pieces. 'Is *this* what you're going to sell? To *women*?'

Blake said angrily, 'If we can't make profit with quality, we've got to—'

'Is this *what you're going to sell? To* women*?'*

5

'*Who* can't make profit with quality?' King asked. 'Maybe the Old Man can't, and maybe you can't, but—'

'Doug, this is business, business.'

'I know it's business! It's *my* business, the business I love! Shoes are part of my life, and if I make garbage, my life will smell!'

'I can't continue to hold stock in a company that's going downhill,' Blake said.

'Then sell out! What the hell do you want from me?'

'Careful, Doug,' Benjamin said suddenly. 'We could vote you out of your job.'

'Go ahead, vote me out,' King said.

'If you find yourself out in the street—'

'Don't worry, I won't be out in any street.' King threw the pieces of red shoe on the table, and started to walk towards the door.

'If you helped me to become president,' Benjamin said, 'you would get a much bigger salary. You could . . .' He stopped. 'Where are you going? I'm *talking* to you.'

'This is my house,' King said. 'I've had enough of this meeting, and your plans, and I've had enough of *you*! So I'm leaving. Why don't you leave too?'

Benjamin's narrow face was red with anger. 'You don't want me to be president of Granger, is that it?' he shouted.

'That's it exactly,' King said.

'Who the hell do you think *should* be president?'

'You just think about it,' King said, and went out of the room. There was a long silence. Then Benjamin walked over to Pete Cameron, who was standing at the bar.

'What's he planning, Pete?'

'I have no idea.'

'Don't play the innocent, Pete,' Benjamin said. 'We offered him a plan, and he refused us. He must be feeling strong to do that. What's he feeling so strong about?'

'Why don't you ask *him*?'

'Don't get clever with me, boy. What's your salary? Twenty, twenty-five thousand? You can do better than that, Pete.'

'Can I?'

'What is it? A deal with the Old Man? I want it smashed, and the man who helps me smash it could find himself taking King's job. Do you know my home telephone number, Pete?'

'No.'

'Westley Hills 4-7981. Will you remember it?'

'I've been Doug's assistant for a long time,' Cameron said.

'Then it's time for a change. Give me a call.'

'You're very persuasive,' Pete said. 'It's a good thing I'm an honest man.'

'Yes, it's a good thing,' Benjamin said dryly. 'That's Westley Hills 4-7981.'

Stone put on his hat and said, 'If that bastard King thinks he can . . .' He stopped, as Diane King came into the room. The men stared at her. Then Stone raised his hat and said politely, 'Mrs King.' He went out of the door, followed by Benjamin and Blake.

Immediately, Diane said to Cameron, 'What did they do to Doug?'

2

'Why would anyone want to steal radio parts?'

Douglas King's house lay just within the 87th Precinct. It was on the edge of the Precinct, in Smoke Rise, the most expensive area of the city.

The River Harb lay to the north of Smoke Rise. To the south was Silvermine Road, the home of people who, although they were rich, were not rich enough to live in Smoke Rise. Anyone walking south from Silvermine Road came first of all to a noisy area of brightly lit all-night restaurants and stores, then to Ainsley Avenue, where it was still possible to imagine that it had once been fashionable to live. Then came Culver Avenue, and now it was clear that the walker was arriving at the poorer parts of the city. After the short burst of colour of the Puerto Rican area around Mason Avenue, Grover Avenue looked grey, dirty and very poor.

The 87th Precinct building was on Grover Avenue.

Detective Meyer Meyer was at his desk on the second floor, making notes as the man sitting opposite him spoke. The man was called David Peck. He owned a store on Culver Avenue which sold radio parts, he told Meyer.

'I sell mainly to hams,' Peck said.

'Hams?'

'Yeah, hams. Not like hams you eat. By hams I mean people who build their own radios as a hobby. They use them to talk to other hams. You'd be surprised how many hams we've got in this city. It's a good business to be in.'

'I guess so, Mr Peck,' Meyer said. 'So what's your problem?'

'Well,' Peck said, 'someone busted into my store.'

'When was this?'

'Last week.'

'Why did you wait until now to report it?'

'He didn't take much. I thought I'd just forget it.'

'What makes you report it now?'

'The crook came back.'

'When?'

'Last night.'

'And this time he stole a lot of equipment, is that right?'

'No, no. This time he took even less than last time.'

Meyer Meyer breathed out slowly. He was a very patient man. Growing up with parents who had given him that name, he had had to learn to be patient. Being the only Jewish boy in the area, he had had to learn to fight with his intelligence, not with his hands.

Patiently, now he asked, 'Tell me, Mr Peck, what did the thief steal the first time he broke into your store?'

'An oscillator,' Peck said.

'What does an oscillator cost?'

'I sell them for fifty-two dollars and thirty-nine cents.'

'And that's all he took the first time?'

'Yes.'

'And what did he steal last night?'

'Little things. More bits of equipment. Batteries. The whole lot isn't worth more than twenty-five dollars.'

'So why are you reporting it this time?'

'Because I'm afraid he'll come back a third time and clean out the store. It's possible, you know.'

'I know it is, Mr Peck,' Meyer said. 'Thank you for reporting this to us. We'll keep a special watch on your store.'

A crime involving radio equipment worth seventy-five dollars does not appear to be a very important crime. In the 87th Precinct crimes like that happen every day of the week. Why get excited about this one? – unless you are a very patient detective called Meyer Meyer, who has a very good memory.

Meyer studied his notes, and then walked over to a desk on the other side of the room. Steve Carella was sitting there, typing up a report.

'Steve,' Meyer said. 'I just had a guy in here who . . .'

'Shhh, shhh,' Carella said, and continued typing until he had finished the page. Then he looked up.

'Okay?' Meyer said.

'Tell me.'

'I had a guy in here who owns a radio parts store on Culver Avenue. It's been broken into twice. The first time the thief stole an oscillator, whatever that is. The second time he stole a few other small radio parts. Now, I seem to remember . . .'

'Yeah,' Carella said, searching through the piles of paper which covered his desk. 'Where the hell's that list?'

The list gave details of five break-ins at radio parts stores. Each time only a few pieces of equipment had been stolen.

'Think it's the same thief?' Carella asked.

'Sure as hell looks that way to me,' Meyer said.

'Anyway, it's not very serious.'

'I suppose not.' Meyer paused and scratched his head. 'You don't think he's a Russian spy? Why would anyone want to steal radio parts?'

'Never try to understand crooks,' Carella said. 'You'll go

crazy if you try to do that.'

'Still,' Meyer said, 'all that equipment. Seven break-ins. What does it mean, Steve?'

'Search me,' Carella said, and he began typing again.

'Never try to understand crooks.'

3

'Jump down and attack! Take him by surprise!'

Diane King was not what Hollywood calls a beautiful woman. She was, however, an attractive woman. In fact, Diane King was an extremely attractive woman.

She stood there in her luxurious house, a woman of thirty-two, wearing narrow black trousers and a white shirt. She had a towel around her shoulders, and a silver streak in her black hair. Again she asked Pete Cameron, 'What did they do to Doug?'

'Nothing,' Cameron said. 'What did you do to your hair?'

'Oh, it was Liz's idea,' Diane said. 'What was all the shouting about?'

'Is Liz still here?' Cameron asked, with interest in his voice.

'Yes, she's still here. I hate these meetings! Why did Doug rush upstairs past me? He didn't even see me!'

'He saw *me*,' a voice said, and Liz Bellew came into the room. Diane King was not beautiful. Liz Bellew was. She had blonde hair, blue eyes and a full mouth. Even dressed simply in a skirt and sweater, she looked like a million dollars. On her left hand she wore an enormous diamond ring.

'No man runs past me without saying hello,' she said.

'So hello, Liz,' Cameron said. 'What have you done to Diane?'

'You mean her hair. Isn't it wonderful?'

'I don't like it. I think she's pretty enough without it.'

'I'll wait and see if Doug likes it,' Diane said. 'Where is Doug? What's he doing up there?'

12

'He's only making a phone call,' Liz said.

'Is he in trouble, Pete? That look on his face . . .'

'Don't you know that look?' Liz said. 'My Harold wears it all the time. It means he's about to murder someone.'

'Murder!' Diane said. 'Pete, what happened?'

'Nothing. They offered Doug a deal, and he turned them down.'

'My Harold would have kicked them out of the house,' Liz said.

'That's just what Doug did.'

'Then prepare yourself for a murder, Diane,' Liz said.

'I'm always prepared,' Diane said, with a troubled look in her green eyes, 'but they seem to happen so often these days.'

'Well, Diane,' Cameron said. 'That's business. Dog eat dog.'

'Anyway,' Liz said, 'murder can be fun. Lie back and enjoy it.' She smiled at Cameron, and he smiled back at her. The two had been secret lovers for years. Surprisingly, perhaps, this had never stopped Liz from loving her highly successful husband, Harold, with all her heart, or Pete Cameron from spending most of his time thinking about work.

Diane poured herself a drink. '*Is* Doug planning something?' she asked Cameron.

'Yes, I think so.'

'I thought he might—'

'Might what?' Doug King asked, as he came into the room.

'Did you make your phone call, tycoon?' Liz asked.

'I couldn't get through.' He kissed Diane, then looked at her and said, 'Honey, you've got egg in your hair!'

'Sometimes I wonder why we bother,' Liz said, annoyed.

'Don't you like it, Doug?' Diane asked.

13

King spoke carefully. 'It's okay, I guess.'

'*Okay*?' Liz said. 'You'll have to do better than *okay*, Doug!' She looked at her watch. 'I must go. I promised *my* tycoon I'd be back at four.'

'You're late already,' Cameron said. 'Have a drink before you go. One for the road.'

'I really shouldn't,' Liz said. 'You'll have to persuade me.'

'I'll persuade you all right. I know what you like.'

Their eyes met. Fortunately, at that moment the telephone rang, and Diane picked up the receiver. 'Hello?' she said. Then she handed it to Doug. 'It's your call from Boston.'

Cameron looked up from the drinks he was mixing. 'Boston?' he said.

'Is that you, Hanley?' Doug asked. 'How's it all going?'

'It's going fine, Doug. We're getting there,' said the voice in Boston.

'Listen, we've got to act fast, get the deal all tied up today.'

'Today! He wants to keep five per cent of the stock, Doug. I'm doing my best, but I don't think—'

'I need that five per cent as much as I need the rest, Hanley,' Doug said. 'I don't care how you do it, but get that deal for me today!'

'Well, I'll try, Doug, but—'

'Don't just try, Hanley. Succeed. I'll be waiting for your call.'

He put the phone down and turned to Cameron. 'Pete, you're going to Boston.'

'I am?' Cameron said, handing Liz her drink.

'Lucky boy!' she said. 'I just love the shops in Boston.'

'You're going to Boston with a big fat cheque,' King said. 'You're going to help me make the biggest deal of my life!'

14

'What's it all about, Doug?'

'I'll tell you later,' King said. 'Not yet. Telephone the airport and see when the next flight leaves. Use the phone upstairs. I want to keep this one free for Hanley to phone back.'

Cameron smiled at Liz as he left the room.

King clapped his hands together sharply. 'Oh boy!' he said. 'Are those guys going to get a big surprise! Trying to involve me in their rotten little plan! Can you believe it, Diane?'

'Excuse me, Mr King,' a voice said.

The man who had come into the room was only thirty-five, but he looked older. He was Charles Reynolds, the Kings' chauffeur. Looking at him, you felt that there was something weak about the man, and also something terribly sad. It was not a surprise to learn that his wife had died, leaving him to bring up his young son alone.

'What is it, Reynolds?' King asked, a little impatiently. He was fond of Reynolds, but not of the man's weakness.

'I only wanted to know, sir . . . is my son, . . . is Jeff here, sir?'

'That's a question for *Mrs* King,' King said.

'He's upstairs, playing with Bobby,' Diane said.

'Oh fine. I hope I'm not bothering you, but it's getting a bit cold. If they go outside, I think he'll need a coat.'

'Don't worry, Reynolds,' Diane said. 'I've already given Jeff one of Bobby's sweaters.'

'Oh, thank you, ma'am. I never seem to be able to decide—'

'You'll probably be driving Mr Cameron to the airport later,' King interrupted.

'Yes, sir. When will we be leaving, sir?'

With a loud scream, Bobby King, wearing a blue sweater, rushed down the stairs and burst into the room, closely followed by Jeff Reynolds, who was wearing a red sweater. Both were eight years old, both blond, and at first sight they could have been mistaken for brothers. Taking no notice of the adults, they ran towards the door.

'Hey!' King shouted to his son. 'Stop there!'

'What is it, Dad?'

'Where are you going?'

'Outside to play. Let us go! We're in a hurry!'

'Why? What are you playing?'

'We're playing cowboys and Indians, Mr King,' Jeff said. 'We take turns. The Indian has to hide in the woods, and then the cowboy has to find him.'

'Don't go too far from the house, Bobby,' Diane said.

'I won't, Mom.'

'Who's the Indian now?' King asked.

'I am!' shouted Jeff.

'Quiet, son,' Reynolds said, 'and take good care of that nice sweater Mrs King lent you.'

'Oh, sure,' Jeff said. 'He won't catch me, Dad, don't worry.'

'Oh, won't he?' King interrupted. 'You'd *better* catch him, Bobby, if you're a true son of mine! What's your plan, boy?'

'Plan, Dad? Just chase him and catch him, that's all.'

'Never chase the other man, son,' King said. 'I can see you need help.'

'Oh Doug, just let them go and play before it gets dark,' Diane said.

'I will,' King said, smiling, 'but first the boy needs some professional advice.' He whispered to Bobby, 'Climb a tree and watch him. When you know what he's going to do, jump down and attack! Take him by surprise!'

'We're not allowed to climb trees in this game,' Bobby said.
'Do anything you like, son, as long as you play to win.'
'Doug, what are you saying to the boy?' Diane said.
'Only the facts of life,' Liz answered.
'Why don't *I* get any help, Dad?' Jeff asked his father.
'Well,' Reynolds said hesitantly, 'you could hide behind a

'Plan, Dad? Just chase him and catch him, that's all.'

17

rock and keep still. Then he won't be able to find you.'

'If you don't move, there's no game,' King said. 'What's the point of playing?'

'Just go and play the way you want to, boys,' Diane said coldly. 'Go on now, have fun.'

With a shout, the two boys rushed out of the house.

'A madhouse, just like my own home,' Liz said.

'I'll have the car ready when Mr Cameron needs it, sir,' Reynolds said.

When he had gone, Diane said, 'You shouldn't have told Bobby that, Doug. What do you want him to grow up to be? A wild animal?'

'Mmmm, yes,' King said. 'Just like his mother, with sharp teeth, and—'

'Doug, I'm serious!'

'So is he,' said Liz. 'He's trying to make love to you, Diane.'

'I'm sorry you think this is a joke,' Diane said. 'I don't think it's so funny. All this jumping on people and taking them by surprise. It's just what you do in business. It's what you're doing with this Boston thing. You're getting so *hard*, Doug, so merciless to other people.'

King laughed. 'Me? Merciless? Am I hard and merciless, Liz?'

'Of course not. You're a darling.'

'Just because I get things done, Diane, you call me hard. Honey, there are people who sit and people who *do*, and if I hadn't been a *doer* all these years, you wouldn't be in this house, and driving that car, and wearing that—'

'He's right, Diane,' Liz said, waving the hand with the diamond on it.

'Of course I am. I just need to make my *wife* understand—'

'I'm sure you know just how to do that,' Liz said. 'Have fun.'

When she had left, there was silence for a moment. Then King said softly, 'Diane?'

'What?'

'I'm sitting in a tree, looking down at you, and I'm warning you . . . I'm getting ready to . . . jump down and attack you!'

He took her suddenly in his arms. 'Let me go!' she said. 'If you think you can . . .' Then he kissed her.

'You're beautiful, Diane, did you know that? Especially with that new silver streak in your hair.'

'You should be ashamed of yourself.'

'I know.' He kissed her again. After a while, she pulled herself free. 'Pete's still here, Doug,' she said shyly.

'I'll send him to the airport early. Give me a minute. I just have to ring Hanley, then I'll get rid of Pete, and we'll be alone.'

He went to the phone and picked up the receiver. Somebody else was on the line, and he recognized the voice as Cameron's.

'. . . yes, George,' Cameron was saying, 'that's what I'm trying to tell you. Well, I thought you'd like to know . . .'

King pushed a button on the phone, putting him through to another line. 'Funny,' he said.

'What's the matter?' Diane asked.

'Pete's on the other line. I got the idea he was talking to . . .' King stopped and then said into the phone, 'Get me Oscar Hanley at the Hotel Stanhope in Boston. Okay, call me back.'

'How about a drink, Diane, before . . .'

The door burst open, and Bobby rushed in. 'I forgot my gun, Mom!' he shouted. 'I've got to get it! Jeff's already hiding in the woods! I've got to find a tree to climb, Dad!'

'Still ready to jump down and attack, Doug?' Diane said.

19

* * *

The man was hidden, waiting to attack. He was dying for a cigarette, but he could not have one. He watched the chauffeur cleaning the Cadillac. He looked at his watch. He looked at the sky. It would be dark soon. Good.

He wondered if Eddie was still with the car. He wondered if everything was okay at the house. He wondered if their plan would work. Then he began to worry, and he needed a cigarette more than ever.

'Easy now,' he told himself. 'Just take it easy.'

Then he saw the boy coming towards him through the woods. 'Hello, sonny,' he said.

* * *

It was getting dark in the city, that special October dark that smells of wood smoke and autumn leaves. It starts to get cold in October. People hurry home, wanting their dinner, wanting the companionship of their loved ones.

It will be dark soon.

It will be good to get home before it grows dark.

4

'We've got your son'

In the Kings' living room the telephone rang. Douglas King picked up the receiver and said, 'Hanley?'

A voice on the other end said, 'Who?'

'Oh, excuse me,' King said. 'I was expecting another call. Who is this, please?'

'All right, Mac,' the voice said. 'I'm going to make this short and—'

'There's nobody called Mac here,' King said. 'You must have the wrong number.'

He put the receiver down. Cameron was standing there, watching him.

'Not Hanley?' Cameron said.

'No. A wrong number. Talking about wrong numbers, Pete . . .'

'Yeah?'

'Were you talking to George Benjamin a little while ago?'

'Yes, I was.'

'Why?'

'To tell him I won't be at the sales meeting tomorrow.'

'You didn't tell him you were going to Boston, did you?'

'No. Should I have told him?'

'Hell, no!'

The phone rang again. 'That will be Hanley,' King said, walking over to the phone.

'I'd better call Bobby in,' Diane said. 'It's getting dark.'

21

'Wait a minute, honey. Let me take this call first,' King said. 'Hello, Hanley. Did you get what I wanted?'

'I got it,' Hanley said in a tired voice. 'Exactly what you wanted. Including the five per cent of the stock he wanted to keep. How soon can you get a cheque to me?'

'I'll send Pete Cameron with the cheque on the nine o'clock plane. Can you meet him at the airport?'

'Okay, Doug.'

'Oh, and Hanley?'

'Yes, Doug?'

'Good work, boy!'

King put down the receiver. 'Now we move!' he said excitedly. 'Pete, phone the airline and get a seat on the nine o'clock plane.' He pushed a button on the phone, picked up the receiver again and said, 'Reynolds, come over here. As fast as you can.'

'Is everything fixed?' Cameron said. 'Can you tell me about it now?'

'Now it's all fixed, I'd even tell Benj . . . No, no, I guess I wouldn't tell him.' He laughed, and then walked quickly to the bar and poured himself a drink.

'I'd better get Bobby,' Diane said. 'Look how dark it's getting.'

'Wait a minute, Diane. Don't you want to hear this? Bobby's safe enough. He's just outside his own house!'

'Well . . . all right. But I really . . .'

'You heard Benjamin say I had thirteen per cent of the voting stock, didn't you, Pete?'

'Right.'

'Wrong.' He paused. 'I've been buying stock for the last six years. I've got twenty-eight per cent of it.'

'Doug, that's wonderful!' Diane said.

'So why am I going to Boston?' Cameron asked.

'There's a guy there who owns some voting stock I want to buy. Hanley's been working on him for the last two weeks, and now he's finally ready to sell it to me.' He sat down at a desk and began to write a cheque.

'How much stock is it?' Cameron asked.

'Nineteen per cent.'

'Whaaat!'

'Add it up. Nineteen and twenty-eight makes forty-seven. Enough to make me president of Granger! I'll run the company my way, and I'll make the shoes I want to make!' He tore the cheque from the book and gave it to Cameron. 'Take a look at this,' he said.

Cameron took it and gave a low whistle. 'Seven hundred and fifty thousand dollars,' he said.

'Doug, where did you get . . .?' Diane started to ask.

'Everything we own is tied up in this deal, Diane. This house, everything.'

'The house? Doug . . .!'

'I can't lose, Diane. Nothing can stop me now.'

'Who are you buying the stock from?' Cameron asked.

'A guy who bought it a few years ago. He—'

'Who? Who is he?'

They stopped talking, as Reynolds came into the room, ready to drive Cameron to the airport.

'I must get Bobby in,' Diane said. She went to the door, and started to call, 'Bobby! Bobby!'

The telephone rang. King picked it up. 'Hello?' he said.

23

'Listen to me, King,' a voice said. 'Don't put the phone down this time. This is no joke.'

'What?' King said. 'What did you say?'

'We've got your son, King.'

'My *son*? What are you talking about?'

'Bob-by!' Diane called. 'Will you *please* come in now?'

'Your son,' the voice said. 'We've kidnapped your son.'

'You've taken my son? If this is some kind of joke—'

Diane turned from the door. 'Doug!' she screamed. 'What did you say? What's happened to Bobby?'

King waved a hand at her, wanting her to be silent, as the voice went on, 'Now listen and listen hard. I'll only say this once. The kid is safe. He'll stay safe if you do what I say. Get five hundred thousand dollars. Get it by tomorrow morning. We'll call you then and tell you what you have to do. Don't go to the police, King. Do you understand?'

'Yes, I understand.' Desperately, he searched for an idea, some way of trapping the caller.

'Okay, then,' the voice said, 'five hundred thousand dollars in—'

King put the receiver down, cutting off the call. 'Pete,' he shouted. 'Get on the kitchen phone. Call the police. Bobby's been kidnapped, and we've had a five hundred thousand dollar ransom demand.'

'No!' Diane screamed. '*No!*'

'Then call the phone company. Tell them I hung up on the bastard.'

'Why did you do that?' Diane shouted. She ran to the door and screamed into the darkness, 'Bobby! *Bobby!*'

'I hung up so that he'll call back,' King said. 'Then the phone

24

company may be able to find out who made the call.' He took Diane in his arms. 'We'll get him back, darling,' he said. 'Please, Diane, try not to worry. I'll give anything they want, a million dollars if they ask for it.'

Cameron rushed in from the kitchen. 'The police are on their way,' he said. 'The phone company say you must call them on another line as soon as he rings again.'

'Okay,' King said. 'Reynolds, will you—' He stopped suddenly, as the front door burst open.

'Were you calling me, Mom?' Bobby King said, as he came into the house.

Diane ran to him, fell to her knees and threw her arms around him. 'Hey, Mom!' he said, surprised. 'What's the matter?'

King stared at his son. 'How on earth . . .?'

'I don't want to play with Jeff any more,' Bobby said. 'I climbed a tree like Daddy told me, but I couldn't find Jeff anywhere. He won't play with me! I don't even know where he is!'

There was a moment of shocked silence. The name was on everyone's lips, but it was the boy's father who spoke.

'Jeff,' Reynolds whispered. 'Jeff!'

5

'We've got the wrong kid!'

There were two kinds of cases that Steve Carella did not like. He did not like cases which involved very rich people or cases which involved children. Now, sitting in Douglas King's enormous, luxurious living room, talking about a kidnapped child, Carella felt bad. He didn't want to be here, but he had no choice.

He sat in King's room, feeling troubled and asking questions, while Meyer Meyer stood with his back to them, looking out at the River Harb.

'Let me get this clear, Mr King,' Carella said. 'The boy who was kidnapped is *not* your son, is that right?'

'That's right,' King said.

'But when the kidnapper asked you for the ransom money, he thought he had your son.'

'Yes.'

'Has he called you again?'

'No.'

'Then he may still believe he has your son,' Carella said.

'I don't know what he believes,' King said angrily. 'Why do I have to answer all these questions? I am not the boy's father, and I—'

'No, but you spoke to the kidnapper.'

'That's true, Mr Caretta.'

'Carella.'

'I'm sorry. Carella.'

'Was it a man? The person who called.'

'It was a man,' King said.

'Did he say "*I* have your son" or "*We* have your son"?'

'I don't remember. And I don't see why it's important. *Somebody* has Jeff Reynolds, and all these stupid questions—'

'Exactly, Mr King,' Carella said. '*Somebody* has the boy, and we want to know who that *somebody* is. We want to know who has the boy so that we can get him back safely. That's important to us. I'm sure it's important to you, too.'

'Of course it is!' King said sharply. 'Why don't you call in your chief – somebody experienced in this kind of case? A boy's life is in danger! Local cops can't handle this.'

'Lieutenant Byrnes is on his way now, Mr King,' Carella said. 'He's boss of the whole 87th Precinct. First we need to know a little more about—'

'Excuse me, Steve,' Meyer said. 'I'd better go and get a description of the boy. I ought to talk to his father.'

'Yeah,' Carella said. 'Where is Mr Reynolds, Mr King?'

'In his apartment. Over the garage. He's taking this badly.'

'Do you want me to speak to him, Meyer?' Carella asked.

'No, no, I'll do it,' Meyer said, giving King a quick look as he turned to leave the room. 'I think you have your hands full here.'

'Now, Mr King,' Carella started again. 'Did you notice anything unusual about the man's voice? An accent, or—'

'I'm sorry, Mr Caretta,' King said. 'I refuse to play this little game any longer.'

'My name is Carella, and what game do you mean?'

'This nonsense about how the man spoke. What difference can it possibly make? How will any of this get Jeff back to his father?'

Carella did not look up from the book he was writing in. He kept telling himself that it would really not be a good idea for him to hit Mr Douglas King in the mouth. Quietly, politely, he asked, 'What do you do for a living, Mr King?'

'I run a shoe factory. Is this another of your important questions?'

'Yes, it is. I don't know anything about shoes, Mr King. They're just things I put on my feet. I wouldn't dream of going into your factory and telling your workers how to make shoes.'

'I understand what you're saying,' King said dryly.

'You understand part of what I'm saying, Mr King. The part that is warning you . . .'

'*Warning* me!'

' . . . warning you to let me get on with my job. The other part of what I'm telling you is this. In case you have any doubts about

'What do you do for a living, Mr King?'

28

this, let me tell you that I am a good detective, a *hell* of a good detective. I know my job, and if I'm asking you questions it's because I have a good reason to ask you those questions. Now do we understand each other, Mr King?'

'I think we understand each other, Mr Caretta.'

'My name is Carella,' Carella said flatly. 'Did the man have an accent?'

* * *

Reynolds sat on his bed, making no attempt to hide the floods of tears that were running down his face. Meyer watched him, and wished he could put his arm around the man's shoulders, tell him everything would be all right. He could not do that. He did not know whether the boy was alive or dead. All he could do was ask his questions.

'How old is Jeff, Mr Reynolds?'

'Eight.'

'How tall is he?'

'I don't know. I never . . . I don't know. Maybe a little tall. He's a handsome boy. Tall for his age.'

'How much does he weigh?'

'I don't know.'

Meyer breathed in deeply. 'Is he fat, thin, medium?'

'Not too fat and not too thin. Just normal.'

'Is he dark or fair?'

'He has blond hair. Very fair skin. Is that what you mean?'

'Yes. Thank you. What colour are his eyes?'

'Will you get him back?' Reynolds asked suddenly.

Meyer stopped writing. 'We're going to try,' he said. 'We're going to try every way we know, Mr Reynolds.'

The description of Jeff Reynolds was phoned to the 87th

29

Precinct building, and then sent out to the police forces of fourteen states. The message which followed it immediately was about a grey Ford car. It had been stolen.

* * *

The grey Ford bumped along the rough road which led to the lonely farmhouse. Sands Spit was not the kind of place where many visitors chose to spend their summers. In winter it was freezing and completely deserted.

The Ford stopped at the farmhouse and a young man in his late twenties stepped out and ran to the door. He knocked three times, then waited.

'Eddie?' a woman's voice asked.

'It's me, Kathy. Open the door.'

The door opened. 'Where's Sy?' the girl asked.

'In the car. He'll be here in a moment. Ain't you got a kiss for me, Kathy?'

'Oh, Eddie, Eddie,' she said, and threw herself into his arms. A woman of twenty-four, with the pretty but hard face of one whose life has never been easy, Kathy Folsom kissed her husband warmly, with a love which came straight from her heart.

'Are you all right?' she asked him. 'Did everything go all right? I've been worrying so much about this job. I just kept thinking, it's the last one; please don't let anything go wrong.'

'Everything went fine. Give me a cigarette, honey.'

She watched him as he lit the cigarette, a tall, good-looking man in a white, open-necked shirt.

'I was listening to the radio,' she said. 'I thought they'd say something about the job. I mean, a bank . . .' She paused. 'It went all right, didn't it? There was no trouble?'

'No trouble. Only, Kathy, you see, we didn't—'

She kissed him again. 'You're back,' she whispered. 'That's all that matters.'

'In here, kid,' a voice said, and Jeff Reynolds half fell into the room. The man who had pushed him through the door, Sy, laughed as he said, 'Home, sweet home, kid! It ain't much, but it's ours!'

'Where's my gun?' Jeff said, as Kathy stared at him, not understanding what was happening.

'The boy wants his gun,' Sy said, smiling.

Kathy kept staring at Jeff. 'Who . . . who the hell . . .?' she began.

Sy laughed. 'Oh, Eddie, look at the surprise on her face! What a girl!'

'Let me talk to her, Sy,' Eddie said.

'Where's the gun?' Jeff said. 'Come on, I have to get home soon.' He turned to Kathy. 'Have you got the gun?'

'What gun? Who is this kid?'

'Where's your manners, Miss Kathy?' Sy smiled. 'This boy is our guest, and—'

Immediately, she turned to her husband. 'Eddie, who—?'

'I don't think you've even got a gun,' Jeff said.

Sy opened the door to one of the bedrooms. 'Come on, kid, the gun room is this way,' he said.

Kathy waited until the door closed behind them. Then she said, 'Tell me about it, Eddie.'

'It's what it looks like.' He could not raise his eyes to look at her. 'We've kidnapped the boy.'

'Have you gone completely crazy?' she asked.

'Take it easy, Kathy. Try and take it easy.'

She lit a cigarette with fingers that shook. 'All right. I'm

31

listening. Tell me everything.'

'We've kidnapped the boy. We're asking for a ransom of five hundred grand.'

'You said it was a bank job,' Kathy said.

'I was lying. We never went near a bank.'

'Don't you know how serious this is, Eddie? You're crazy! You could go to the electric chair for this!'

'Calm down. Don't get excited.'

'Who is the kid?' Kathy asked.

'Bobby King.'

'And who's Bobby King?'

'His father is a big guy in Granger Shoe. You know the company, Kathy. They make those expensive shoes.'

'Yes, I know it.' She was silent for a moment before she said softly, 'Why didn't you tell me what you were planning?'

'I didn't think you'd agree to it.'

'Of course I won't agree to it!' she shouted. 'Get that boy out of here! Take him back where you got him! His parents must be going mad with worrying about him. How could you do a thing like this?'

'Shut up!' Eddie shouted. Then he said more gently, 'Kathy, we'll get five hundred grand from this job. We'll go to Mexico, just like you said you wanted to.'

'I don't want the money. I won't touch it. And I won't go to Mexico. You said this would be the last job. A bank, you said, just a bank, not taking somebody's child, not a dirty, rotten kidnapping!'

'We didn't hurt the kid,' Eddie said. 'He's fine.'

'Is he?' Kathy said. 'What's Sy doing to him?'

'He's all right. Sy promised to show him a real gun. That's

how we got him to come with us. Try to understand, honey.'

'I don't want to understand this,' she said. 'What the hell gave you the idea . . . ?'

'I just got it. Sy and me worked on the plan together. This is safer than a bank job. We just borrow a kid, and get five hundred grand when we give him back.'

'*Borrow* a kid, Eddie? Who said that, you or Sy?'

'I told you, we both had this idea—'

'You're lying, Eddie. It was Sy's idea, wasn't it?'

'No! Well . . .'

'It was, wasn't it?'

'Well, it was. But it's a good idea, honey. We'll go to Mexico. I'll make something good of my life there, Kathy, you'll see. I'll really be something – me, Eddie Folsom. Won't that be great, honey?'

'Oh, Eddie, Eddie,' she said, looking at him sadly. 'Don't you even realize what you've done?'

'Bang!' Jeff shouted, as he ran into the room carrying a gun. Sy was just behind him. 'The kid likes guns,' he laughed. 'Play with the gun, kid. Get to know it.'

'Sy, is that gun loaded?' Kathy asked, frightened.

'Would I give a loaded gun to a little child?' Sy asked innocently. 'What do you think I am, a bad guy?' He turned to Eddie and said, 'Time to turn on the magic box, professor.'

Eddie looked at Kathy, but she would not meet his eyes. 'Sure, Sy,' he said, and pulled a cloth off a heap of radio equipment, which stood on a table in the corner of the room.

'Watch the professor, kid,' Sy said, as Eddie turned the huge radio on, pushing buttons and watching needles move from side to side. 'You sure found yourself a smart guy, Kathy.'

'Why don't you leave my husband alone?' Kathy said. 'Why did you get him into this rotten thing?'

'He came willingly,' Sy said. 'I ain't forcing him.' A high sound came from the radio. 'The magic box speaks, kid.'

'Hey, that's great!' Jeff said. 'Where did you get it?'

'I built it,' Eddie answered.

'That must be really hard to do.'

'Not so hard,' Eddie said, trying not to sound too pleased.

'Clever husband you got yourself, Kathy,' Sy said. 'That's why the little woman loves you so much, Eddie. And you learnt it all in reform school, didn't you?'

'Stop it, Sy,' Kathy said.

'Want to build radios like Eddie here, and have all the girls running after you?' Sy asked Jeff.

'I sure do!'

'Okay, this is what you have to do. When you're fifteen years old, rob a store. Then they'll send you to reform school. That's where Eddie got his education. Me, kid, I had to get my education in the rope factory.' He laughed. 'Is it coming, professor?'

Suddenly, voices came from the radio.

' . . . *accident at Morrison and North Ninety-eight. Car 303 . . .*'

They were listening to the police talking on their radios.

'Are you going to take me home now?' Jeff asked.

'I'm busy, kid,' Sy said.

'*Car 207, car 207, go to Smoke Rise, house of Douglas King . . .*'

'Hey!' Jeff said, excited. 'He said Douglas King!'

'Do you really expect this plan to succeed, Sy?' Kathy said.

'Sure, I do. And all because of the professor here, and his radio. I love Eddie and his radios! I love this job! It's going to do great things for all of us! Tell her, Eddie, tell her all about it!'

'Sy, she's not interested,' Eddie said.

'I'm interested in anything Eddie does,' Kathy said softly.

'Sure you are. The little woman,' Sy said. 'Okay. Here's what we did. We called King and told him we wanted five hundred grand . . .'

Jeff said, 'Did you say you called—?'

'Shut up, kid. We told him to get the money ready by tomorrow morning. Then, in the morning, we call again . . .'

'Are you talking about—?' Jeff started.

'I said shut up, kid, before you get hurt!' Sy shouted angrily.

Jeff stared at him, surprised, and then frowned.

The radio broke the silence in the room.

' . . . *all cars, all cars. Here's the story on the Smoke Rise kidnapping. The missing boy is eight years old, fair hair, wearing a red sweater. The boy's name is Jeffry Reynolds . . .*'

'What?' Eddie said.

'That man said my name,' Jeff said, surprised.

' . . . *son of Charles Reynolds, chauffeur to Douglas King . . .*'

'What's he talking about, Sy?' Eddie said. His face was white with terror.

'They're lying,' Sy said. 'It's some kind of trick.'

'How can it be? We've got the wrong kid!'

'He ain't the wrong kid!'

'If he is,' Kathy said calmly, 'you've done all this for nothing. We're all in trouble for nothing.'

'This kid is Bobby King,' Sy said. 'Sure he is.'

'Me?' Jeff said, puzzled. 'I'm not Bobby.'

'Shut your mouth, kid.'

'Let him talk,' Kathy said. 'What's your name, sonny?'

'Jeff.'

'He's lying!' Sy shouted.

'I am not!' Jeff shouted back at him. 'I don't like you! I'm going home!'

He started to walk to the door. Sy caught him roughly by the arm and pulled him back. He stood very close to the boy, and there was no laughter in his voice as he said, 'What's your name? Your *real* name?'

'I'm not Bobby,' said Jeff.

6

'This little boy is in big trouble'

A cold wind blew off the River Harb, along the road which led to Douglas King's house. It froze the fingers of Parker, Hawes and Kronig, the three detectives who were working there, working in the cold and the dark. Any detective – any *man* – would rather be at home on a night like this, at home with a good book, a good woman or a good bottle of whisky. To be honest about it, a bad book, a bad bottle of whisky, even a bad woman would be better than this cold.

But the job had to be done. The marks made by a car, a match thrown in the road, a cigarette end – anything could be important in a case like this. Anything could lead to the missing boy.

At last they found it. Small marks in the frozen mud by the side of the road. The marks made by the tyres of a car, a car that has been turned around in a hurry.

* * *

Reynolds was watching Cassidy, the man from the telephone company, as he worked. Cassidy was putting an extra telephone into Douglas King's house for the police to use. He was putting in a wiretap, too, so that it would be possible for the police to trace the kidnapper's call – if he called again.

'I thought we'd hear something by now,' Reynolds said.

'Don't worry, mister,' Cassidy told him. 'When they find out they got your kid by mistake, they'll just leave him in the street somewhere. The kid's all right, believe me.'

'If they leave him in the street, he'll get lost,' Reynolds said. 'He won't know where to go.' He turned to Carella, who had just been talking on the phone. 'Did they have any news, Detective Carella?'

'I was talking to Auto Squad,' Carella said. 'I've asked them to check all stolen cars, in case the kidnappers had stolen the car they used.'

'He's worried about the kid,' Cassidy said. 'I keep telling him it'll be all right. Any minute now the kid could walk in the door, not a hair on his head harmed.'

'Do you think so?' Reynolds asked Carella.

'Well . . .' Carella started, and then the doorbell rang. It was Parker, happy to be in at last from the freezing cold.

'We've found a tyre mark,' he told Carella. 'Kronig's making a cast of it now. Not that it will help anyone. It's all a waste of time, if you ask me. The kid's probably dead already.'

Carella quickly touched him on the arm, and looked across the room at Reynolds, but it seemed that the chauffeur had not heard Parker's remark.

'They ought to take all kidnappers out and shoot them,' Cassidy said. 'The electric chair's too good for guys that can steal a man's kid from him. Well, I guess I've finished here. I'll just test my phones and go.'

'Have you heard anything yet, Detective Carella?' King said, as he came into the living room with a coffee cup in his hand. Diane and Cameron were directly behind him.

'Not yet, Mr King,' Carella said.

'Well, what's the problem? Are your men really looking for the boy? Do they have a description of him?'

'Yes sir, they do.'

'Do they know he may be somewhere out on the street? Some member of the public may find him. Is anybody taking phone calls from the public?'

'It's all taken care of, sir.'

'All this,' King said, 'extra phones, wiretaps, it all seems a waste of time to me. There's even a policeman outside my son's bedroom door!'

'That's right,' Carella said. 'We're taking no risks. We have no idea what the kidnappers will do next, you see.'

'I don't think they have any choice,' King said. 'They'll have to let the boy go free.' He caught sight of Reynolds, still standing miserably on the other side of the room. 'Go to the kitchen and get something to eat, Reynolds.'

'I'm not very hungry, Mr King.'

'Go on, man, you've got to eat. Jeffry will be back before you know it.'

When Reynolds had gone, Diane said, 'Mr Carella, the kidnappers know by now that they've got the wrong boy, don't they?'

'They should know, Mrs King. It's been on all the radio and TV stations, and in all the newspapers.'

'You don't think they'll harm him, do you?'

'Of course they won't!' King said sharply. 'As far as they're concerned, it's just a business deal that's gone wrong.'

'They may harm him, Mrs King,' Carella said calmly. 'You know that sometimes a thief will beat up a man for not having any money to give him.'

'That would be senseless,' King said. 'I'm sure they'll let him go as soon as they know he's not my son. These people are not stupid.'

'You don't have to be smart to be a kidnapper,' Carella said. 'You just have to be hard-hearted.'

'We hadn't thought of that,' Cameron said. 'They may hurt him before they let him go. It's a possibility.'

'Yes,' Carella said. 'There's another possibility, too.'

* * *

'My name is Jeffry Reynolds,' the boy said.

Sy took him roughly by the arm. 'You're lying!'

'I'm not lying. Hey, let go that sweater, will you? It doesn't belong to me!'

'You lying little bastard!' Sy shouted, and pushed Jeff hard, throwing the boy across the room.

Kathy screamed, and took a step towards the boy.

'What's your father's name?' Sy shouted.

'Ch-Charles.'

'Where do you live?'

'At Mr King's place.'

'Don't call him Mr King!' Sy shouted. 'You know he's your father!'

'No!' Jeff said desperately. 'He's *Bobby's* father!'

'Shut up!' Sy shouted. 'Take off that sweater!' He pulled it over Jeff's head roughly. A slow smile spread over his face. 'If you're called Jeff, why is the name in your sweater Robert King?'

'That's Bobby's sweater!' Jeff said. 'Mrs King lent it to me.'

'Tell the truth!'

'I *am* telling the truth!'

Sy stood there calmly, a small, neatly-dressed man who badly needed a shave. Then suddenly, violently, he hit the boy across the face.

'Eddie, stop him!' Kathy shouted, as Jeff rushed into her arms, crying, 'I *am* Jeff Reynolds, I am, I am!'

'Stop it, Sy,' Eddie said. 'The kid's frightened. Let me see the sweater.' He looked at the name in it. 'It says Robert King, Kathy.'

'He says he borrowed it. Is that so hard to accept?'

'Yeah,' Sy said. 'With five hundred grand to lose, it is hard to accept.'

'Let's take the boy home,' Kathy said softly.

'Sure!' Sy said. 'And go straight to prison. He knows us. He could lead the police to us!' He turned to Eddie. 'We want that money, don't we?'

'I don't want it!' Kathy screamed. 'I don't need it!'

'Well, I do,' Eddie said softly. 'I want that money. I wasn't born in Smoke Rise, with a rich father. When the hell did anyone ever give me anything? This is my one chance to have something. I want a place of my own, in Mexico, a place for you and me, Kathy.' There were tears in his eyes as he spoke.

'But he's the wrong boy!' Kathy said.

'No,' Eddie said. 'No, he ain't.'

'Eddie, you know he is.'

'When you think about it,' Sy said softly, 'what difference does it make? Maybe we got the wrong kid. Maybe this is the chauffeur's boy. We can still ask King for the money.'

'He won't pay, Sy,' Eddie said.

'He'll pay, all right,' Sy said, 'because if he won't, then this little boy is in big trouble.' He paused and smiled at Jeff. 'And I don't think Mr King would want blood on his hands.'

7

'I want to talk to you about the ransom'

Lieutenant Peter Byrnes was on his way to Smoke Rise. A child had been kidnapped. Byrnes had a son of his own, and he knew the pains and pleasures of fatherhood. To him, kidnapping a child was the worst crime in the world. Death was the correct punishment for a kidnapper.

Seeing a light on the dark road by King's house, Byrnes told his driver to stop. He got out of the car. 'Kronig, Hawes, how are you boys?' he said. 'What have you got there?'

'We've got a tyre mark,' Kronig said. 'It's a good one. I'm making a cast of it.'

'Fine, fine,' Byrnes said, looking around. 'Can you bring that light here a minute, Hawes?'

'What is it, Lieutenant?'

'Let's take a look at this rock here.'

* * *

In King's living room the telephone rang.

'Wait!' Carella shouted, as King moved to answer it. Carella picked up the wiretap equipment. 'Mr Cameron,' he said, 'get on the new phone. If this is the kidnapper, tell the phone company to start tracing the call immediately. Okay, Mr King, you can answer it now.'

King picked up the phone.

'Hello?'

'King?'

'This is Mr King.'

42

Cameron said into his phone. 'We've got him on the phone now. Start tracing the call.'

'All right, King,' the voice said, 'listen. We don't care whose kid this is. We heard the radio message, and we don't care. He's still alive and well, and we want that money. Get it tomorrow morning, or the kid will be dead by the end of the day.'

'You want . . .?' King started, but the voice had gone.

'Hell, I was afraid this would happen,' Carella said. He picked up his coat and hurried out of the room.

Diane looked puzzled. 'Is Jeff all right?' she asked her husband.

'He's fine.'

'Are you sure?'

'Of course I'm sure, Diane!'

'I'll go and tell Reynolds,' she said.

'Diane!'

'Yes?'

'They want me to pay the ransom. They know they've got Jeff, but they still want me to pay. They want me to . . .'

'We'll do whatever they say. Thank God Jeff's all right,' Diane said. As she left the room, King stared after her, frowning.

'We're dealing with professionals,' Cameron said. 'He knew we would try to trace the call. That's why he made it so short.'

'Yes,' King said. He seemed to be thinking hard.

'Why are they still asking you to pay? Hell, if you pay them, it's the end of your Boston deal.'

'Yes. Yes, it is.'

The doorbell rang. It was Meyer. 'I just saw Carella,' he said. 'He's gone outside to talk to Lieutenant Byrnes.'

'The kidnappers called again,' King said. 'They want me to

43

pay the ransom.'

'What do you mean? Do they know they got the wrong kid?'
'Yes.'

'And they still want you to pay?' Meyer shook his head. 'First time I ever heard this one,' he said. 'Crazy! But who ever said kidnappers have to be normal human beings?'

'What are our chances of getting the boy back, Detective Meyer?' King asked. 'Do you think they are good?'

'I don't know,' Meyer said. 'He could be dead already.'

'In your opinion,' King said slowly, 'will paying the ransom help the boy at all?'

'If he's alive, it will certainly help him,' Meyer said. 'If he's dead, nothing can help him, but we could use the dollar bills to catch the kidnappers.'

'I see.'

'Doug, the boy's still alive!' Cameron said. 'Your money will keep him alive, remember that!'

Diane came into the room from the kitchen. 'I think Reynolds is in shock,' she said. 'He's just sitting at the table, staring at nothing.' She turned to King. 'Doug, have you called the bank yet?'

'No, not yet.'

'Isn't it time—?'

'Mommy?'

They all turned, and saw Bobby King, in his night clothes, standing on the stairs.

'What is it, darling?' Diane said.

'Why is there a policeman outside my room?' Bobby asked.

'Just to make sure everything is all right,' Diane said.

'Because of what happened to Jeff?'

'Yes, Bobby.'

'Daddy,' Bobby said, 'are you getting Jeff back?'

'What?' King said. 'I'm sorry, son, I didn't hear . . .'

'Your Daddy's taking care of everything,' Diane said. 'Come on, let's get you back into bed.'

'I want Daddy,' Bobby said.

'Doug? Will you put Bobby to bed?'

'Sure,' King said, although he was clearly thinking about something else. 'Come on, Bobby.'

'Poor Bobby,' Diane said to Cameron. 'He doesn't really understand what has happened. He only knows that his friend has gone, and I think he feels guilty. I feel like that myself.'

'You have no reason to feel guilty,' Cameron said. 'Doug will pay the ransom, and . . .'

'Yes, but I *do* feel guilty,' Diane said. 'I almost feel that my own son is missing.' She paused. 'Detective Meyer,' she said, 'could you come and talk to Reynolds? You could explain to him what the police are doing to get Jeff back. All this is such a terrible shock for him.'

'Sure,' Meyer said.

When he was alone in the living room, Cameron lit a cigarette, stood listening for a moment, and then quickly went to the telephone and dialled a number.

'May I speak to Mr Benjamin, please?' he said. 'This is Peter Cameron. Yes, I'll wait, but please hurry.'

At last a voice said, 'This is George Benjamin.'

'Pete Cameron. I have to make this fast. Do I still get Doug's job?'

'I offered it to you, didn't I? Do you want it in writing?'

'Yes, I do. The Boston thing I told you about. It's a stock deal.

45

Doug's planning to buy nineteen per cent of the voting stock. He already owns twenty-eight per cent. He's smarter than you thought he was, George.'

'Twenty-eight . . .' There was a long silence. 'Then we can't vote him out. What the hell can we do?'

'The only way to do it is to get the Old Man on your side,' Cameron said. 'Tell the Old Man that Doug is trying to do a deal behind his back.'

'How will that help? If he buys that stock, he'll have forty-seven per cent of it. We can't get rid of him. Hell, he can get rid of us!'

'*If* he buys the stock. Have you heard the news on the radio?'

'This kidnapping nonsense?' Benjamin said. 'What difference can that make? The kid isn't King's son.'

'No, but they've asked him for the ransom. If he pays, he can't afford to buy that extra nineteen per cent of the stock. If he pays, the Boston deal's off.'

'Will he pay?' Benjamin asked.

'Sure he will. Meanwhile, I'm trying to find out who he's dealing with in Boston.'

'Good work, Pete,' Benjamin said.

'Thanks, George. Take my advice, go talk to the Old Man.'

'I'll do that. And I won't forget this.'

'I know you won't. I have to go now, George.'

Cameron smiled to himself as he put down the receiver, and lit another cigarette. He was still smiling when the doorbell rang, and he went to answer it. A small man, dressed completely in black, was standing there.

'Mr King?' the small man said.

'No. I'm Mr King's assistant.'

'I would like to see Mr King, please. You may tell him that Adrian Score is here to see him. On personal business.'

Cameron took Score into the living room and went upstairs to tell King about his arrival. 'I don't know anyone called Score,' King said.

'He says it's personal business.'

'I'll come down. Bobby's gone to sleep.'

King came into the room where Score was waiting. 'What do you want?' he asked.

'To do business, Mr King.'

'Isn't it a bit late in the evening for that?'

'It's never too late to do business.'

'What kind of business are you talking about, Mr Score?'

'Kidnapping, Mr King.'

The room went silent.

'Do you want your son back?' Score asked.

'My son hasn't been kidnapped.'

Score laughed. 'Well, we can tell the newspapers it's not your son, but we know the truth, don't we? Let me ask you again, do you want the boy back?'

'Of course I do.'

'Now, I know where he is, Mr King, and for a small fee I can help you to get him back.'

'Who has the boy, Mr Score?'

'As one businessman to another, Mr King, I must ask for a cash payment before—'

'Before what, Score?' a voice said. 'Before you disappear, leaving another unhappy family behind you?' Meyer Meyer had come quietly into the room and had heard everything Score had said. 'Mr Score and I have met before,' Meyer went on. 'Now get out of here before I arrest you for giving false information, Score.'

'I must protest strongly,' Score said. 'I am an honest businessman, providing a service—'

'Out!' Meyer shouted. 'Now!'

'I can get your boy back!' Score shouted, but he went, all the same.

'Who is he?' King asked Meyer.

'A rotten crook,' Meyer said. 'And there are plenty of other sick characters like him, Mr King, who will try to make money

'Out!' Meyer shouted. 'Now!'

48

out of this kidnapping. I don't know how he got past our men at your gate. There's only one thing I do know, Mr King.'

'What's that?'

'I'm glad I'm not back at the office answering the telephones right now.'

* * *

Lieutenant Byrnes walked into King's living room and said, 'Hello, Steve, how's it going?'

'All right, sir,' Carella said. 'Mr King, this is Lieutenant Byrnes.'

'How do you do, sir?' Byrnes said, and he shook hands with King.

'How does it look, Lieutenant?' King asked.

'Not too bad, not too good. I understand they're asking you to pay the ransom, Mr King. That's bad. But we may have found something good outside.'

'What's that?'

'We're getting a clear cast of a tyre mark, and we've just found some paint from the same car on a rock. This car was turned around in a hurry outside your house. Detective Carella asked Auto Squad to get me a list of stolen cars. I've just received the list and now, with a little luck, we'll soon know which car we're looking for.'

'How will that help you find the boy?' King asked.

'It will give us something to look for. I know it doesn't sound like much, but we haven't got much to help us, and anything is better than nothing. Once the money has been delivered, we can note down some of the numbers on the dollar bills. That will help us to trace them later. And when we get the boy back, perhaps he'll be able to describe the kidnappers.'

'Unless he's dead,' King said flatly.

'If he's dead, there wouldn't be any sense in continuing, would there, Mr King?'

'None at all,' King said.

'I want to talk to you about the ransom, Mr King,' Byrnes went on. 'You haven't called your bank yet, have you?'

'No, I haven't.'

'Good. I'd like to speak to them when you do, and—'

'I'm afraid I won't be able to help you, Lieutenant,' King said.

Byrnes stared at him, puzzled. 'I don't understand,' he said.

'I won't be talking to my bank. I'm not going to pay the ransom.'

'You're . . .' The room went silent. 'Of course, it's your decision, Mr King,' Byrnes said. 'Nobody can force you to pay it.'

'What are you saying, Mr King?' Carella said, frowning. 'You have to pay the ransom! That boy hasn't got a chance unless—'

'Shut it, Steve,' Byrnes said.

'I don't *have* to do anything,' King said slowly. 'I'll tell you again, I'll tell the kidnappers and I'll tell anyone else who wants to listen. I am not paying the ransom. Do you understand? I am *not* paying the ransom.'

8

'I'm taking you out of here'

Jeff Reynolds turned over in his sleep, and the blanket which covered him fell free of his shoulder. Kathy Folsom went to the bed and covered him again. Eddie Folsom lit a cigarette. In the bathroom, Sy was singing at the top of his voice.

Eddie was listening to police calls on the radio he had built.

'Sy,' he called, 'Sy, did you hear that?'

Sy, dressed only in his trousers, came out of the bathroom, where he was shaving. 'What's the matter?' he asked.

'The police are blocking all the roads! They're stopping every car! How can we use the car tomorrow?'

'What are you getting so excited for?' Sy said. 'I'll be driving, right? In an ordinary old car, right? We've changed the number plates. Nobody will know it's a stolen car. If the cops stop me, I'll tell them I'm on my way to work.'

'What about after we get the money?' Eddie said. 'How are we going to leave? They'll still be watching.'

'We won't have the kid with us,' Sy said. 'There's nothing to worry about. Let me finish shaving, will you?'

When he had closed the bathroom door, Kathy said, 'Eddie, what will happen to the boy after Sy gets the money?'

'We'll leave him here. We'll call King to tell him where the boy is.'

'That sounds so dangerous, Eddie. Oh, Eddie, let's get out of here now, before it's too late!'

'Stop worrying, honey,' Eddie said. 'You've got to believe

51

what Sy says, Kathy. He's been a good friend to me.'

'A good friend!' Kathy said. 'I think he wants to kill the boy, Eddie.'

'Aw, come on, Kathy! Sy doesn't want to kill anyone! All he wants is his share of the money.'

'What about you?' she asked. 'What do you want, Eddie?'

'The same thing. The money.'

'And what are you willing to do to get that money?'

'What the hell are you talking about?' Eddie said angrily. He looked around for another cigarette, found an empty packet and called to Sy, 'Got any cigarettes, Sy?'

'In the car!' Sy shouted from the bathroom. 'Let a guy shave in peace, can't you?'

Eddie started to walk toward the door.

'Tell me, Eddie,' Kathy asked again. 'What will you do to get that money? Is kidnapping okay? Then why not murder? Will you stop at murder, Eddie?'

'This is crazy, Kathy.'

'Sy is planning to kill that boy,' she said, 'and I have to know what you think.'

'Can't you just leave me alone?'

'No, Eddie. I have to know.'

'All right, all right,' Eddie said. 'Look Kathy, I want to have something . . . be something . . . you know? I want to go to Mexico, I want to have money, a lot of money. I never had anything, Kathy. I . . . I don't want to be poor, to be dirt, anymore, okay?'

'Okay, but . . .'

'Honey, don't ask me any more questions. Don't ask me why I'm doing this. It's the only thing I can do.'

'It isn't, Eddie,' she said. 'We could leave now. We could leave the boy somewhere, and go to Mexico, just the two of us.'

'I . . . I don't know,' he said. 'I need a cigarette, Kathy.'

'Eddie, tell me.'

'Leave me alone!' he shouted. 'I'm getting out of here!'

'Where are you going?'

'To the car for those cigarettes, and . . . and then I'm going for a walk.'

'I'll go with you.'

'I don't want you with me! Leave me alone!'

The door closed, leaving her alone with the sleeping child. In the bathroom, Sy began singing again. Kathy looked at the bathroom door, then at the boy. She had decided what she must do.

Quickly, she touched Jeff on the shoulder and whispered, 'Jeff! Wake up, Jeff!'

He sat up immediately. 'What is it?' he said. 'What? What?'

'Quiet!' she whispered. 'Listen to me, and do what I tell you to do. I'm taking you away from here.'

'You're taking me home?' Jeff said excitedly.

'Keep your voice down!' They could hear Sy singing, and the sound of running water. 'I can't take you home, but I can take you out of here. I'll have to leave you somewhere. Someone will find you. You'll get home. But you have to help me. We have to move fast. Do you understand?'

'Yes,' Jeff whispered. 'Are . . . are they going to kill me?'

'I don't know. We won't give them the chance.'

'Is Eddie your husband?'

'Yes.'

'He's not so smart,' Jeff said, 'but I don't think he would hurt me.'

53

Kathy was silent.

'You're pretty,' Jeff said.

'Thank you. Now come on. Put that sweater on. It's very cold outside.' She pulled the sweater over his head. 'When we get to the road, we start running,' she said. 'Do you understand?'

'Yes. I'm a good runner.'

She put on her coat and led him silently towards the door. Slowly, she turned the handle.

'Wait!' Jeff said. 'I want my gun!' He broke away from her and rushed back into the room. The gun was on a table. As he picked it up, it sent a heavy ash-tray crashing to the ground. The two of them froze, unable to move.

The bathroom door opened. 'Well, well,' Sy said as he came out. 'Where do you think you're going? Where's Eddie?'

'He went to the car for cigarettes,' Kathy said.

'So you thought you'd run off with the boy, did you?' Sy said. He went to the door and locked it. 'Nice trick, honey! Now take off your coat.'

Kathy hesitated.

'Get it off before I tear it off you!' Sy shouted.

She threw the coat onto the bed. Sy walked up to her slowly, reaching into his pocket. Suddenly, she could see a knife in his hand. 'Listen to me, little lady,' he said, holding the knife up to her face. 'Try that again, and you're going to need a good doctor to put your face together again. Understand? And this little bastard will be dead meat.'

'I'm not afraid of you, Sy,' she said.

'No? You'd better start being nice to me, honey,' he said. 'Maybe I'll forget what you tried to do if you're real sweet to me.' Still holding the knife to her throat, he put his free hand on her shoulder. She tried to pull away from him.

'Hey, open the door!' Eddie called from outside.

Sy put the knife away and Kathy unlocked the door. Eddie came into the room.

'It's a great night,' he said. 'Cold but clear. You can see the stars.'

'That means the weather will be good tomorrow,' Sy said. 'Even the weather is on our side.' He looked at Kathy. 'Nothing can stop us now,' he said. 'We're all going to be rich.' He turned to Eddie. 'Your wife ain't too excited by this job, Eddie,' he said.

'Listen to me, little lady.'

'Tell her about it. Tell her what a beautiful plan we've got.'

'Do we have to talk about it?' Eddie said. 'Let's just do it.'

'I want her to know how great it is. You see, Kathy, we're going to call King in the morning and tell him what to do, and the cops won't be able to stop us or find us. How does that sound, Kathy?'

'Very smart,' she said in a flat voice.

'Yeah,' Sy said. 'Very smart. Nobody will know where we are or what we're going to do, and all because of Eddie and his magic box.' He pointed to the radio equipment. 'Why do you think we took the trouble to rob all those different radio stores? To give Eddie something to play with?'

'I thought that you needed it to listen to police calls,' Kathy said, puzzled.

'Oh no,' Sy said. 'There's more to it than that. This isn't just a radio receiver. Look at those oscillators, that transmitter . . . We've got a big surprise for King and the cops too. Once King starts to do what we want, nobody will know what's happening except him and us. Once he leaves the house with the money . . .'

'*If* he leaves the house,' Kathy said. '*If* he pays the ransom.'

'I'll tell you a secret, sweetheart,' Sy said. 'He'd better leave the house, and he'd better pay the ransom.' He looked at Jeff as he put his hand into his pocket and took out the knife. The boy's eyes were wide with terror.

'He'd *better* pay the ransom,' Sy said softly.

9

'If you don't pay them, they'll kill him'

Lieutenant Sam Grossman was the scientist who ran the police laboratory. It was his job to take the cast of the tyre mark which Kronig had made and the tiny bit of grey paint and to find out what kind of car they came from.

Grossman's job was not always pleasant. Pieces of bodies, hair, blood and bone were things he saw every day. However, he enjoyed his work because he knew that he was helping to send thieves and murderers to prison. Sometimes his job was extremely difficult, but today it was easy. In a very short time he was able to phone Meyer Meyer and tell him that the car he was looking for was a five-year-old grey Ford.

* * *

Meyer took the call from Grossman in Douglas King's living room. While the two policemen talked, King sat silently staring into the fire. He did not look up when Meyer told him that he was going to talk to Byrnes.

He still did not look up when Diane came into the room and stood between him and the fire.

'All right,' she said, so quietly that he could only just hear her. 'Pete told me what you've decided. You can't be serious.'

'I am serious, Diane.'

'I don't believe you.'

'I'm not paying. Start believing it, Diane. I'm not paying.'

'You have to pay,' Diane said.

'I don't have to do anything. They're just crooks. Why should

57

I play their game?'

'Game? It isn't a game. There's a little boy involved. If you don't pay them, they'll kill him.'

'He may be dead already.'

'They told you he was alive,' Diane said. 'You know they did.'

'They may kill him even if I do pay.'

'And if you don't pay, they will certainly kill him.'

King got up from his chair. 'Would you like a drink, Diane?' he asked.

'No, I would not,' she said. 'Doug, how can you play with a child's life like this?'

'Why should I care about this kid at all?' King said. 'What is Reynolds doing to help his son? Nothing! Why should *I* pay for *his* son?'

'But he's just a child!'

'I don't care. He's nothing to me. Do you know, Diane, I don't even like the kid! Why should I be responsible for him?'

'They meant to take Bobby,' Diane said. 'That makes you responsible for him.'

'Not at all. It just makes him unlucky,' King said. 'In any case, I haven't got the money they're asking for.'

'You *have* got it, Doug,' she said. 'Don't lie to me.'

'I need all the money I've got for this deal. I can't give that away. Don't you understand?'

'Yes, I understand completely,' she said. 'Your business deal means more to you than a child's life.'

'The business is my life,' King said. 'It's everything I've worked for. It's a part of me, Diane. Don't you realize that?'

'To hell with the business!' she shouted. 'I don't care about Granger Shoe. I don't care whether you own it or not.'

'Listen to me!' King said angrily. 'Let me tell you what will happen if I pay that ransom. Benjamin and his friends will get together with the Old Man and throw me into the street. I'll have no job, Diane! I'll be finished!'

'You could start again.'

'Where? How could I? We'd lose everything – this house, the cars, the way we live – it would all go. Why should I do anything? Why can't someone else pay?'

'*You* were asked,' Diane said.

'Why me? Because I've got money? I didn't get it by sitting around watching the world go by! I've worked hard for everything I've got. Why can't Reynolds pay the ransom for his own son? Because he's never worked as hard as I have, that's why! He's sat around doing nothing, and now he wants me to help him. Well, I don't want to help him. I don't want to help anybody except myself.'

'You don't mean that,' Diane said. 'You can't mean that. What's happened to you, Doug? What's happened to the man I love?'

'I don't know what you mean.'

'Maybe it's my own fault,' Diane said. 'All those years, I just stood and watched, as you got harder and crueller and did worse and worse things to people.'

'How could I—?'

'Shut up and listen to me!' she shouted. 'You've destroyed so many men on your way to the top, Doug, and I just watched. You want to destroy Benjamin, too, and the Old Man and throw them into the street. You don't care about anyone!'

'That isn't true, Diane, and you know it,' King said. 'Haven't I always given you what you wanted? Haven't I been a good husband to you and a good father to Bobby?'

'The business has always meant more to you than we have,' she said. 'You've given us money, a home, food, but you've never given us anything of yourself. Only the business matters to you, and now you're ready to murder a little boy to get what you want!'

'Murder? No, Diane . . .'

'It is murder,' she said. 'You can call it by other names, but it is murder, and this time I won't stand by and watch you do it!'

'What do you mean? What are you talking about?'

'If you don't pay the ransom, I'm leaving you.'

'Leaving?'

'I'm taking Bobby and I'm getting out of this house.'

'Come on, Diane, you don't know what you're saying. You—'

'I know exactly what I'm saying, Doug. Pay the kidnappers, because I don't want to be anywhere near you if you don't. I won't live with somebody who's rotten and dirty, who—'

'Honey, honey,' he said, reaching out his hand to her. 'Can't you—?'

'Get away from me!' she screamed. 'Don't touch me, Doug! This time I've had enough!'

'I can't pay,' he said. 'You can't ask me to.'

'I'm not asking,' she said. 'I'm telling. Have the money ready when the kidnappers call tomorrow morning.'

'I can't give it to them,' he said. 'Diane, I can't pay. You can't ask me to.'

But she had already walked out of the room.

10

'You're out and I'm in!'

After a long cold night, the sun was rising, washing the house in golden light. In the bedroom, Diane silently packed clothes into a bag, while Liz Bellew drank coffee and watched her.

'Why are you doing this, Diane?' Liz asked. 'By asking Doug to pay the ransom, you're asking him to destroy his life and yours, too. It doesn't make sense.'

'Doesn't it?' Diane said. 'What would you do if one of your children was kidnapped, Liz?'

'I'd cut off my arm if it would save him,' Liz said.

'And what if my boy – Bobby – was taken, and they asked you for the money?'

Liz drank some coffee. Even at this time in the morning, she looked beautiful. 'Darling,' she said, 'I love you like a sister, but I'm not sure that I would pay all that money to save somebody else's son.'

'I'm surprised,' Diane said.

'Why? Because I'm a mother? I'm only mother to three children, not the whole world,' Liz said.

They were silent for a while, and then Diane said, 'It was good of you to offer me a place to stay.'

'Of course you can stay at my house for as long as you like, Diane,' Liz said, 'but if Doug asks me what I think about all this, I'll tell him that I think you're mad.'

'He already thinks I'm mad,' Diane said. 'He knocked at my bedroom door three times in the night. The last time, I think he was crying, but I wouldn't let him come in. He has to understand that I'm serious. He has to understand that I'm leaving him unless he pays the ransom.'

Somebody knocked at the door. 'Who is it?' Diane asked.

'Me. Pete.'

'Could you go to the door, Liz?' Diane asked.

'Good morning, Mr Cameron,' Liz said, as she opened the door. 'Did you sleep well?'

'Liz!' Cameron said, surprised to see her. 'I didn't know you got up so early in the morning.'

'I always wake up early and ready for action,' Liz said. 'What brings you to a lady's bedroom?'

'A problem. I've got Doug's cheque in my pocket, Diane. What should I do? Take it to Boston or tear it up?'

'You'll have to ask Doug,' Diane said.

'I ought to tear it up,' Cameron said. 'He's going to pay that ransom. I'm sure of it.'

'Why are you sure?' Diane said. 'I don't understand.'

'Look,' Cameron said. 'Let's say I go to Boston and the deal goes ahead. Imagine the story in the newspapers. Douglas King, they'll say, the man who now controls Granger Shoe, the man who refused to save a little boy's life. Hell, they'll tear him to pieces. Nobody will ever buy a pair of Granger shoes again!'

'I hadn't thought of that,' Diane said.

'But Doug will think of it. That's why he'll pay.'

There was a cough, and they all turned towards the door. Douglas King stood there. His eyes were red and tired, but he had a determined look on his face.

'Good morning, Doug,' Cameron said. 'Did you sleep well?'

'No, I didn't sleep well. Diane, why is Liz here?'

'I called her last night, Doug. I'm taking Bobby to Liz's house.'

'I see.' He turned to Cameron. 'When are you leaving, Pete?'

'What? Well I . . . I don't know.'

'What do you mean? Which plane are you on?'

'I didn't ring the airport. I thought—'

'It's not your job to think. I gave you a cheque to take to Boston, didn't I?'

'Yes, but . . . I didn't know whether you still wanted me to . . .'

'Nothing's changed. Go downstairs and call the airport. Get a seat on the next flight to Boston.'

As Cameron left the room, Diane said, 'I guess I'd better finish packing, Liz.'

King stared at her for a moment, and then went downstairs. Cameron was already talking on the telephone. 'The twelve o'clock flight,' he said. 'Fine. The name is Peter Cameron. All right, thank you.'

He put the receiver down. 'Okay,' he said to King. 'We just put a bullet in Jeffry Reynolds' head.'

'Stop it, Pete.'

'It's true. I think this is murder,' Cameron said. 'Doug, listen to me. Please, Doug, let the deal go and save the kid. He's an innocent child, and—'

'When did you start loving innocent children so much?'

'Everyone loves kids, Doug,' Cameron said.

'Especially Pete Cameron, huh? Don't you know that the Boston deal will help you, as well as me? Is Jeffry Reynolds really more important to you than your own success? I find that very interesting, Pete.'

'A child's life is important.'

'More important than this deal, right?'

'No, but . . .'

'More important or less important? Which?'

'Well, I . . .'

'If I pay the ransom, the deal is off. Is that what you want, Pete? Do you want this deal to fail?' King looked at Cameron coldly. 'I don't believe you care if Jeff Reynolds lives or dies. What's really going on here? Have you got plans of your own?'

'Doug, don't be silly.'

'Why did you call Benjamin yesterday? And don't tell me that lie about a sales meeting. What are you planning with him?'

'Nothing.' Cameron gave a weak laugh. 'I'm not planning anything with anybody.'

'Did you tell him about this Boston deal?'

'Boston? No, of course I didn't.'

King stared at him for a moment. Then he picked up the telephone.

'What are you doing, Doug?' Cameron asked.

King did not answer. 'Get me Mr Benjamin,' he said into the receiver. Then, 'Hello, George. This is Doug. How are you, George?'

'I'm fine. Isn't it a little early in the morning for . . .?'

'George, I've been thinking,' King went on. 'That deal you offered me yesterday. I turned it down. Maybe that was a mistake. I think I'd like to accept your offer, George.'

'You're too late, Doug,' Benjamin said. 'You see, I know all about your deal in Boston. And I know that your deal is off because of this kidnapping. You've lost your deal, Mr King, and now you're going to lose your job, too.'

'I see,' King said softly. 'Well, George, I guess I know when

64

I'm beaten, but I hope you won't punish Pete for my mistake. He knew nothing about my plans. He's a good worker, George, and—'

Benjamin gave a loud laugh. 'Don't worry about Pete. We'll take care of him. Pete will be okay with us, Doug. Now I really must go. I'm meeting someone for a game of golf.'

King put the phone down slowly. 'You bastard,' he said to Cameron. 'You told him about Boston. You told him everything.'

'Yes.'

'Everything. You bastard.'

'Yes,' Cameron said, 'I told him everything, and now you're out, Mr King, out! You're out and I'm in! Tomorrow you're out on the street.'

'Not if the Boston deal goes through.'

'You can't do it. You haven't got the guts to kill that kid!'

'Haven't I?' King said. 'But you have, Pete? Is that right? Then we're both bastards, aren't we, both the same.'

Suddenly, he put his hands on Cameron's shoulders and threw him across the room. 'Get out of my house!' he shouted.

'With pleasure,' Cameron said. He took the cheque out of his pocket and tore it into pieces.

'Get out!' King screamed. 'Get out, get out, *get out!*' Even after Cameron had left the house, he was still shouting, '*Get out, get out!*'

11

'The boy needs a hot drink'

The boy was cold. Kathy had given him her coat, but he still felt cold. He wanted a hot drink, hot chocolate, he said, but there was no milk in the farmhouse, and no chocolate.

Kathy sat with her arms around the trembling child, wondering how Eddie Folsom, the man she loved, could possibly be a part of a crime like this. She knew that he was a thief. To Kathy, robbing a bank was not really a crime at all. But kidnapping a child? How could Eddie, a man who had so much good in him, do a terrible thing like that?

And what exactly were they planning to do, Eddie and Sy? Kathy had seen maps and knew that they were going to use the radio equipment. They were going to telephone King and give him some instructions. She could not understand what all this meant.

'Eddie,' she said. 'The boy needs a hot drink. He's cold. Would you go out and get him something, Eddie?'

'Never try to understand women!' Sy said. 'The roads are full of cops and you want to send Eddie out for a hot drink! That really takes the prize, Kathy!'

'One of you has to go out to make the phone call,' Kathy said. 'You'll have to make the call from a store. Won't it look more normal if you buy some things too?'

'She's right,' Sy said. 'Good idea, Kathy.' He said to Eddie, 'When you make the call, get the kid what he needs.'

'Am *I* going to make the call?' Eddie said.

'Why not?'

'No reason. Okay, I'll go.'

'Do you know what to do?' Sy asked. 'Make sure he's got the money first. Tell him to leave the house at ten o'clock sharp. Tell him to go straight to his car. It must be the Cadillac. Be certain to tell him that, Eddie. We don't want him to use the wrong car. Tell him it has to be the Caddy.'

'All right,' Eddie said.

'Tell him to start driving away from Smoke Rise. Say he'll be met by someone with further instructions. Make sure you say he'll be *met*.'

'Who's going to meet him?' Kathy asked. 'You?'

'Nobody,' Sy said, and he laughed. 'Tell him he'll be watched all the time, and if the police are following him we'll kill the boy.'

'Okay,' Eddie said. 'What do you want me to buy, Kathy?'

'A packet of hot chocolate and some milk. Get some cookies, too.'

He kissed her and said, 'I'll be back soon.'

'Be careful, Eddie.'

'Good luck, kid,' Sy said. 'Here's the phone number.' He gave Eddie a piece of paper.

Eddie went out and got into the car. Sy listened as he drove off down the road. Then he locked the door. 'Alone at last,' he said to Kathy, and he laughed.

* * *

Every policeman sees some horrible sights, and Steve Carella, too, had some bad memories. As soon as he saw Charles Reynolds come into the room, he knew that he would never be able to forget what was about to happen. He wanted to close his eyes, but he could not.

Reynolds looked lifeless, a defeated man. He stood there patiently, and waited for Douglas King, his employer, to notice him.

At last King looked up. 'What is it? What do you want, Reynolds?' he said.

Reynolds took a step towards King. 'I want to ask you to pay the ransom for my son, Mr King,' he said.

'Don't ask me,' King said, and he turned away.

'I have to ask you, Mr King,' Reynolds said. 'Don't you see that? I've never begged in my life, but I'm begging you now. Please, Mr King. I'm talking to you as one father to another. Please save my son.'

'I can't help you. I can't help Jeff.'

'I don't believe that, Mr King. You can save him. Who else can I ask?'

'You're asking me to destroy my own life,' King said. 'Do you understand that? I can't do it.'

'What do you want me to do?' Reynolds said. 'I'll do anything. I'll work for the rest of my life for nothing.'

'Don't talk nonsense. How can—'

'Do you want me to get down on my knees, Mr King? Shall I get down on my knees and beg you to save Jeff?'

He fell to his knees. Carella had to look away.

King was trembling. 'Get up, man,' he said.

'I'm on my hands and knees,' Reynolds said, 'begging you, Mr King, begging you, please, please, save my son.'

Carella saw King's eyes close for a moment. Then he said, 'Please get up, Reynolds. Could you please leave me alone? Could you do that? Please?'

Reynolds got quietly to his feet. He turned and walked slowly out of the room. Douglas King stared after him.

'Do you feel rotten, Mr King?' Carella asked. 'Because that's what you are. A rotten bastard.'

'Look here, Carella. I don't want to listen to that—'

'Oh, go to hell, Mr King!' Carella said angrily.

'What's the matter with you, Steve?' Byrnes said, coming into the room. 'Stop that now.'

'Yes, sir.'

'Get up, man.'

'I've just been on the telephone,' Byrnes said, 'checking our list of stolen cars, and, sure enough, there it was. A five-year-old grey Ford. They'll have changed the number plates, though . . .'

He stopped, as Liz Bellew came down the stairs. She was carrying a bag, and holding Bobby King by the hand.

'Good morning,' she said. 'Any news yet?'

'I'm afraid not, ma'am,' Byrnes said.

'Daddy,' Bobby said, 'is Jeff back yet?'

'No, son. He isn't.'

'I thought you were getting him back,' Bobby said. There was a long, uncomfortable silence. Carella hoped that he would never see the look that was on Bobby King's face on the face of his own son.

'Come on, Bobby,' Liz said. She said to King, 'He's coming over to my house, Doug.'

'Where's Diane? Did you talk to her?'

'Yes, but it's no good. Give her time, Doug. Just be patient.'

'*Why* aren't you getting Jeff back, Dad?' Bobby asked, but Liz pulled him towards the door, and then they were gone.

'I think I should explain,' King said. 'I know that my refusal looks—'

The telephone rang. King stopped speaking, and Carella rushed to the wiretap equipment. 'Answer it, Mr King,' he said. 'Keep him talking for as long as you can.' Byrnes picked up the other phone.

'What . . . what shall I tell him?' King said.

'Tell him you've got the money,' Byrnes said. 'It's our only chance.'

'Answer it! Answer it!' Carella shouted.

'Hello?' King said.

The voice that replied was not the same one he had heard before.

'Have you got the money, Mr King?'

'Keep him talking,' Byrnes whispered.

'Well, yes. I mean, I have most of it.'

'What do you mean, most of it? We told you—'

'The rest of it will be here soon. Five hundred thousand dollars is a lot of money, you know. And I didn't have much time to get it. They're bringing the rest from the bank. It should arrive in half an hour.'

'All right. Fine. Now listen. I'm only going to say this once. You will leave the house at ten o'clock sharp. Carry the money

'Keep him talking,' Byrnes whispered.

71

in a plain box. Go to the garage and get into the black Cadillac. It must be the black Cadillac. Do you understand?'

'Yes, I understand,' King said.

'Hurry, hurry!' Byrnes whispered into the other phone.

'You will drive away from the house, and away from Smoke Rise. You will be watched. Don't take anyone in the car with you, and don't allow the police to follow you. If you are followed, we will kill the boy. Do you understand that?'

'Yes.'

'You will continue driving until someone meets you with instructions. That is all you have to know. Goodbye, Mr—'

'Wait!'

'Keep him talking!' Byrnes said. 'They've traced the call to Sands Spit!'

'What do you want, Mr King?'

'When do we get the boy back? How do we know he's still alive?'

'He's still alive.'

'Can I talk to him?'

'No. Goodbye, Mr King.'

'Wait! You—'

'He's gone,' Carella said. 'His voice sounded different this time. I don't think it was the same guy that called before. Good work, Mr King.'

'Thank you,' King said dully.

* * *

Eddie Folsom had finished his telephone call. Now he had some shopping to do. 'Give me a packet of hot chocolate and a bottle of milk,' he said, 'and a box of those cookies there.'

12

'That five hundred grand has got to be ours!'

Kathy was worried. She walked up and down the room, looking out of the window, and lighting one cigarette after another.

'Where is Eddie?' she said. 'Shouldn't he be back by now?'

'He'll be back,' Sy said. 'Remember, you told him to get chocolate for the kid as well as make the call.'

'When he gets back,' Kathy said, 'what are you going to do?'

'Nothing. Not until just before ten o'clock.'

'And what will you do then?'

'Don't worry about it. Everything will be fine, and we'll all be rich as hell. You know why? Because Sy Barnard is planning this, not some small-time punk like your Eddie.'

'He's not a small-time punk!'

'No?' Sy said. 'So he's a real big-shot. How did you meet such a big-shot?'

'We just met,' Kathy said. 'That's all.'

'But you knew he was a crook?'

'Yes,' she said, 'but it didn't matter to me. He's a good man. He only does this because it's the only thing he knows. I know he's a good man really.'

'Why did you marry him?'

'I love him,' Kathy said.

'When are you going to let me go?' Jeff asked. He was lying on the bed, with Kathy's coat over him.

'Shut up, kid,' Sy said. He turned to Kathy. 'Why worry about Eddie? There's other fish in the sea. Bigger, smarter fish than

Eddie.'

'He's my husband. I love him.'

'Love! That's just for teenagers. There's no such thing.'

'You're mistaken. You just don't know,' Kathy said.

'One thing I do know. Your Eddie is just a cheap crook, and he'll never change. It's too late now for that.'

'It's not too late. Once this is over . . .'

'Once this is over there'll be another job. And another.' He paused and looked at her. 'Listen, let's have a drink.'

'No, thanks.'

'What's the matter? Don't you drink?'

'I don't want any. Where's Eddie?'

Sy picked up a bottle and drank from it. 'You know what your trouble is?' he asked her. 'You worry too much. You don't know how to live. Come on, have a drink.'

'Oh, leave me alone,' she said. 'I don't want a drink.'

'Okay,' Sy said. 'Stand here and worry if that's what you want to do. I can think of better ways of killing time.' He walked closer to her, his eyes on her sweater. 'Eddie ought to buy you some new clothes. A girl like you needs nice things, not this old sweater.'

'Thanks,' Kathy said dryly.

'Know what I think?' Sy went on. 'You're wasting your time with a punk like Eddie. A pretty little thing like you needs someone who knows a bit about the world, someone who—'

'Shut up, Sy,' she said.

'Aren't you hoping the cops will catch Eddie? You never wanted to do this job, did you? All you do is worry about whether the kid's okay, whether we're going to hurt him.'

'Shut up, *shut up!*'

Sy looked at Jeff. 'You're the lucky one, kid,' he said. 'The

74

lady really cares about you. And she cares about Eddie. But not old Sy, that's for sure.' He raised the bottle. 'I'm drinking to you, kid,' he said. 'How about that, you little bastard?'

Jeff said nothing. He was trembling from cold and fear.

'Answer me,' Sy said. 'Ain't you got no manners, boy? Come on, talk. The cops are out there looking for me all over the roads because of you. I want to know what you think about that.'

'I . . . I don't know,' Jeff said.

'You don't know? A smart little bastard like you must have some ideas. Do you want me to go to the electric chair? Is that what you want?'

'Stop it, Sy!' Kathy said. 'Leave the boy alone.'

'Come on, kid, yes or no? Do you want me to get the electric chair?'

'Yes. I mean . . .'

'What? You little bastard!'

'Sy, you're frightening the boy to death!'

Suddenly, Jeff rushed to Kathy and threw his arms around her. He buried his head in her sweater.

'Get your hands off her!' Sy shouted.

Kathy pulled the boy closer. 'That's enough, Sy.'

'What the hell are you saying? No woman tells me what I can do!'

He pulled Jeff roughly from her, throwing the boy across the room. 'There!' he said. 'How about that?'

Kathy hit him, as hard as she could, across the face.

Slowly, Sy took out his knife. 'Okay, baby,' he said. 'You're finally ready to play.'

'Sy, don't . . .'

'Don't what, baby? Don't worry. I won't cut you.' Carefully,

75

he ran the knife up her body, tearing the sweater to pieces.

Kathy moved her hands to try to cover herself.

Sy laughed. 'Get your hands out of the way. I'd hate like hell to hurt you. Now, let's see . . .'

The boy seemed to come from nowhere. He landed on Sy's back like a wild cat, hitting, kicking, pulling Sy's hair. Surprised, Sy turned, tore the boy off him and threw him to the floor. Kathy was at the door, trying to unlock it. Sy caught her by the arm and pulled her to him. 'Maybe you'd better take it easy, baby,' he said. 'Maybe you'll like it better that—'

There was a knock at the door. 'Eddie,' Kathy whispered.

Sy let go of her immediately. 'Put your coat on,' he said. 'Hurry.'

Quickly, she obeyed him.

'One word of this to Eddie,' Sy said, 'and the kid is dead.'

Sy sat down next to the boy. 'Open the door,' he said to Kathy.

'Welcome home,' Sy said as Eddie came into the house. 'Did you get the milk?'

'Yeah.' Seeing the look on Kathy's face, Eddie asked, 'What's the matter here?'

'Nothing,' Kathy said.

'Kathy and I just had a little difference of opinion,' Sy said. 'I got a bit excited, I guess. I'm sorry, Eddie.'

'What was it about? Why are you wearing your coat?' Eddie asked his wife.

'It got a bit cold in here. Are you okay? Were there any police about?'

'I didn't see a single cop,' Eddie said. 'Listen, this is no time for fighting among ourselves.'

'I said I was sorry,' Sy said. 'Get the magic box working,

Eddie. I want to know what the cops are doing.'

'I'll make you some hot chocolate,' Kathy said to Jeff.

The radio suddenly came to life.

'. . . *car used in the Jeff Reynolds kidnapping . . . grey Ford, five years old, number possibly RN 6210 . . .*'

'They know the car!' Eddie shouted. 'We changed the number plate, but they still know it! How can we use it now!'

'Wait,' Sy said. 'Calm down, Eddie. I'll be driving the car, not you. Listen. You said you didn't see any cops when you went to the store. Okay. We're going to use this radio to find out exactly where they are.' He looked at his watch. 'We've got half an hour. Let's hope that the cops send a lot of messages in that time. We can't lose that money now! That five hundred grand has got to be ours!'

13

'Lock him up!'

At ten o'clock in the morning, the front door of Douglas King's house opened and King came out. He was carrying a plain box, filled with old newspapers. He went to his garage, got into the black Cadillac and drove out onto the road.

He seemed to be alone. No police car was behind him. He seemed to be following the kidnappers' instructions exactly.

Nobody who was watching him could know that Detective Steve Carella was hidden in the back of the car, lying on the floor.

'Do you see anything?' Carella asked King. 'Is anyone waving to you from another car? Is there a helicopter overhead?'

'No. Nothing.'

'How the hell are they going to contact you?' Carella said.

* * *

At ten o'clock in the morning, Eddie Folsom turned on his radio equipment. Sy had left earlier, after he had heard enough to know where the police were blocking the roads. Eddie looked at his radio equipment and his maps. Then he looked at his watch. It was ten-three. He would give King another seven minutes. At ten-ten it would start.

* * *

'Can you see anything yet?' Carella asked.

'No.'

'What time is it?'

'Ten-five.'

'Why did you come, Mr King?' Carella asked. 'A detective could have taken your place.'

'I know.' King paused for a moment and then asked, 'Are you married, Mr Carella?'

'Yes.'

'Do you love your wife?'

'Yes.'

'I love mine. She left me this morning. After all these years, she left me. Do you know why?'

'I think so.'

'Because I won't pay the ransom for Jeff Reynolds. You think I'm rotten, I know, but I can't do it. I can't lose Granger Shoe now. It's all I want.'

'If it's all you want, you shouldn't care that your wife has left you.'

'I guess not. I shouldn't care about Diane or Bobby or anybody, should I?'

'No.'

'Then why am I here? What am I doing? I don't understand it myself, Mr Carella. I only know I can't pay the ransom for that boy. It would destroy my life. I'd be poor again. Diane was always rich, Mr Carella. She doesn't know what it means to be poor. I know. I was a poor kid, and I worked hard, I fought, to get what I wanted. Now I'll fight these kidnappers by being here, by doing something, but I'll never pay their ransom. If that means I'm rotten, then I'm rotten, but I won't be poor again. I want my house and my servants and my big car with a telephone . . .'

At that moment the telephone in the car began to ring.

'What's that?' Carella said from the back seat.

'The telephone!' said King. 'The telephone's ringing!'

'My God, that's how!' Carella said. 'Go on, answer it!'

King lifted the receiver. 'Hello?' he said.

'Listen, Mr King,' Eddie's voice said. *'Listen carefully. I'm going to give you your instructions. Don't put the phone down. Nobody can trace this call. I'm using radio, not a telephone. Don't try to contact anyone. Just do what I tell you to. No tricks, please. Do you understand?'*

'I understand.'

Carella climbed over into the front seat, and took the phone from King. He knew the voice the kidnapper could hear over the car phone would be not clear. He hoped that his voice would not sound different from King's. It was a risk worth taking.

'Where are you?' Eddie asked.

'Coming up to North Thirty-ninth where it crosses Culver,' Carella said.

It seemed that Eddie had not noticed the different voice. Calmly, he said, *'Turn left on North Fortieth. Go south until you reach Grover Avenue, then turn left again. When you reach Hall Avenue, let me know. Have you got that?'*

'Yes.' Carella put his hand over the mouthpiece and said to King, 'He's telling us where to go little by little, so that we can't let the cops know what we're doing. These people are smart, Mr King. I wish I knew how to stop them. I just wish I knew.'

* * *

Sy Barnard sat in his car and waited. He was smoking his tenth cigarette in half an hour. Anxiously, he looked at his watch, then at the road again. He felt strangely worried that the plan would go wrong. But how could it?

His car was parked in the woods, completely hidden from the

road by trees. The place was just past a bend in the road. Eddie would tell King to throw the box of money out of the car window, and then to drive quickly on, still following Eddie's instructions. If the police were following, they would have to stay a safe distance behind King, so they would not see when the drop was made. By the time they drove round the bend, King would already have driven away. They would continue to follow, not even knowing that the drop had happened, because King had no way of telling them. Eddie would continue talking to King – leading him, and the police, further and further away – until Sy had picked up the money and driven back to the farmhouse. When Sy stepped through the door, Eddie would stop transmitting.

The plan was beautiful. Why did he feel so worried?

* * *

'*You're going to cross a bridge,*' Eddie said, his eyes on the map. '*You have to pay. Get the money ready. Don't say anything, and don't try any tricks. If you do, we'll kill the boy.*'

Kathy listened as her husband said it.

We'll kill the boy.

Kill the boy.

My husband said those words, she thought. How could he say that?

'*You're coming off the bridge, right?*' Eddie said. '*Now turn left, onto the Highway, and keep driving. Let me know when you pass Exit Sixteen.*'

Kathy looked closely at the map. The farmhouse was clearly marked on it, and King's house. The red line must be the route Eddie was leading King along. What was the meaning of that blue star, then? Of course! The place where Sy was hiding, waiting for King to drop his money. Then Eddie would keep King driving, to get him away from the place and to confuse any followers. So that was where Sy was. Tantamount Road, just around the bend in Route 127 . . .

'Eddie,' she said.

'Not now, Kathy!' he shouted, his hand over the microphone.

'Eddie, let's stop this now. Please. Please.'

'No!' he said.

* * *

Sy looked at his watch.

Come on, Eddie, he thought. Hurry. Let King get here with the money. Let me get back to the farmhouse safely. Please.

* * *

'Please, Eddie,' Kathy said. 'If you love me, I'm asking you to . . .'

'I have to do this, Kathy! I have to!' Eddie said angrily.

'*All right. We just passed Exit Sixteen,*' Carella said.

'Fine. Turn off at Exit Seventeen, and start to drive north,' Eddie said. 'Let me know when you get to . . .'

'The boy is in a farmhouse on Fairlane Road, half a mile from Stanberry!' Kathy suddenly shouted into the open microphone.

'What the hell . . .' Eddie turned to stop her, but he was too late. The words were pouring out of her mouth.

* * *

'*Sy Barnard is waiting in a car . . .*'

'*Kathy, stop it, are you crazy?*'

' *. . . on Tantamount Road, just around the bend in Route 127.*'

'Did you hear that?' Carella shouted.

'I heard it,' King said.

'Get there as fast as you can.' Carella had cut the connection and was already making another call. 'This is a police officer. Get me Headquarters immediately.'

* * *

Sy Barnard was smoking his fifteenth cigarette as the black Cadillac came round the bend in the road.

This is it, he thought. *This is it.*

The car slowed down. He expected to see a box full of money drop out of the window to the ground. Instead of that, the door opened and a man with a gun in his hand jumped out.

Sy started the engine and drove the car at him, but the man fired, hitting one of the tyres and breaking two windows. Sy drove past him onto the road, then left the car and began running into the woods. The man was reloading his gun.

Another man, a big man, jumped out of the Cadillac and began running after Sy. Sy fired at him twice, missing him both times.

'Stop!' the man shouted. 'We know where your friends are!'

'Go to hell!' Sy shouted. He fired several more times, and then the gun was empty, and he threw it away and took out his knife. As the big man came through the trees, Sy held out the knife and said softly, 'Stop there.'

'Like hell!' Douglas King said, and he threw himself on Sy with all the force in his body. The knife tore upwards, through King's coat, running a thin line of blood across his skin, but his hands, strong hands which had once cut leather, were around Sy's throat, and he held him more and more tightly. He did not let go until the knife fell from Sy's hand to the ground and Carella came to help him.

And then it was all over.

King's strong hands were around Sy's throat.

The two policemen found the boy sitting on a bed in the farmhouse, with a blanket around his shoulders.

'Jeff?' one of the men said.

'Yes.'

'Are you okay?'

'Yes.'

'Where did they go?' the other man asked.

'Who?'

'The people who were keeping you here.'

Jeff hesitated for a long time. Then he said, 'There wasn't anybody. Only Sy. I've been all alone here since Sy left.'

'He must be in shock,' one policeman said to the other.

* * *

Jeff refused to change his story.

More surprisingly, Sy Barnard's story was exactly the same as Jeff's. He had worked alone, he said. He knew nobody called Kathy. He did not know what the police were talking about.

'We know you're lying, Barnard,' Carella told him, 'and I don't understand why. Why are you trying to save Kathy? She's the one who told us where to find you. You're not helping yourself, and you're not helping your friends, either. We'll get them. All you're giving them is a little more time.'

'Maybe time is all they need,' Sy said. Suddenly, there was a sadness in his voice. 'Maybe a little time is all anybody ever needs.'

'Lock him up!' Byrnes said.

14

'The case is closed now, but . . .'

Back at the 87th Precinct building, one cold day at the end of November, Steve Carella was typing up his final report on the Jeffry Reynolds kidnapping. He pulled the paper out of the typewriter, turned to Meyer Meyer and said happily, 'Finished!'

'Is it, though?' Meyer said. 'Sy Barnard is in prison, but what about the mysterious Kathy and the man who shouted her name? Where are they now?'

'Out of the country, I guess,' Carella said. 'I wish them luck.'

'What the hell for? They're kidnappers!'

'Jeff Reynolds refused to talk about them,' Carella said. 'I guess that means that they were kind to him. Barnard won't talk either.' He paused. 'Kathy. It's a nice name.'

'She's a sweet girl,' Meyer said. 'She only kidnaps children. Who shall we say some nice things about next? Douglas King?'

'He had some bad moments,' Carella said.

'He asked for them. You know what he was most pleased about when it was all over? The fact that his deal in Boston went through, and he's going to be president of Granger Shoe. Why do the bastards of this world always come out on top?'

'He didn't have to run after Barnard the way he did.'

'Just because a man is brave enough to face a knife, it doesn't mean he can face himself,' Meyer said.

'Give him time. He says he can't change. I think he has to change. His wife went back to him, remember. She must think change is possible for him. She isn't the kind of woman to pick a

86

loser. One day he'll have to pay it, you know.'

'He'll have to pay what?'

'His own ransom,' Carella said. 'The case is closed now, but somehow I feel that it's still open. For a lot of people, Meyer, this case is still open.'

Outside, in the cold, the city waited.

GLOSSARY

ain't *(slang)* short form of *am not / isn't / aren't*

ash-tray a small metal or glass bowl for ash from cigarettes

attractive pretty, nice to look at

Auto Squad police who deal with crimes connected with cars

bastard a rude word to use to someone you dislike

battery a group of electric cells; radios, torches, etc. can run on batteries

big-shot *(informal)* an important, successful person

black (**in the black**) having some money; not in debt

blond(e) *(adj)* golden or yellow haired

bump *(v)* to move in a jerky, uncomfortable way, not smoothly

bust (**into**) *(informal)* to break into a shop or house to steal something

cast a plaster model which shows the shape of something

chauffeur someone who is employed to drive a rich person's car

cookies *(American)* sweet biscuits

cop *(informal)* a police officer

cowboys and Indians a game children play, which involves chasing one another and fighting

crook a criminal

darling a name you call someone you like or love

garbage *(American)* rubbish

golf an outdoor game (popular with business people) in which players try to hit a small ball into a series of holes

grand *(slang)* a thousand dollars or pounds

guts *(informal)* courage

guy *(informal)* a man

headquarters a place from which an organization is controlled

hell *(informal)* a word used to express annoyance, e.g. 'What the hell do you want?'

honey *(American, informal)* a name you call someone you like or love

instructions statements telling somebody what they should do

interrupt to break into a conversation when someone else is talking

Jewish of someone who is a Jew, by race or religion

kid *(informal)* a child

kidnap to take somebody away by force, in order to demand money in return for their freedom

laboratory a room where scientists work on tests

ma'am a very polite way of addressing a woman

mind (on your mind) in your thoughts and causing you to worry

Mom *(American)* a child's word for 'mother'

oscillator part of the electrical equipment for a radio

professor a senior university teacher (also used as a joking name for someone you think is very clever)

precinct an area of a city

punk *(American slang)* an unsuccessful, small-time criminal

ransom *(n)* money paid to a criminal to set free somebody who has been kidnapped

red (in the red) having no money; in debt

reform school a special school for criminals too young to go to prison

scientist someone whose job is connected with a science (e.g. physics, chemistry)

search me *(informal)* I don't know

servant someone employed to work in another person's house

smart *(American)* clever; having or showing intelligence

smash to break

state *(n)* a part of the United States of America, e.g. the state of California

stock (voting stock) *(n)* a share in the control and profits of a business, which is obtained by putting money into the business

store *(n)* a shop

streak a long, thin line of colour

sweater a kind of woollen clothing with sleeves, pulled on over the head

trace *(v)* to find out where something comes from

transmitter equipment that sends out radio signals

tycoon a very rich and important person in business

vice-president the person second to the president of an organization

wiretap making a secret connection to a telephone line in order to listen to people's conversations

King's Ransom

ACTIVITIES

Before Reading

1 Read the story introduction on the first page of the book, and the back cover. Then match these names to the sentences below (sometimes more than one name will match).

Douglas King / Steve Carella / Charles Reynolds / Diane King / Eddie Folsom / Sy Barnard / Jeffry Reynolds / Kathy Folsom

1 She lived in a beautiful house with her husband and son.
2 His father's job was driving cars for a rich businessman.
3 He wanted lots of money, but he didn't want to work for it.
4 He hated criminals – especially kidnappers.
5 His son was in great danger, but he couldn't afford to save him.
6 She knew her husband was planning to do something wrong.
7 He was rich and successful, but he had enemies who wanted to destroy him.
8 His perfect plan went badly wrong.

2 What do you think will happen in the story? For each sentence, choose Y (yes), N (no), or P (perhaps).

1 Steve Carella will arrest all the kidnappers. Y/N/P
2 Eddie Folsom and Sy Barnard will go to prison. Y/N/P
3 Kathy Folsom will decide to help the police. Y/N/P
4 Douglas King will pay the ransom to save Jeffry. Y/N/P
5 Diane King will leave her husband. Y/N/P
6 Douglas King will make the big business deal he wants. Y/N/P
7 Charles Reynolds will find a way to save his son. Y/N/P
8 Jeffry Reynolds will come home safely. Y/N/P

While Reading

Read Chapters 1 to 3, and then answer these questions.

1 Why did Benjamin, Stone, and Blake need Doug King's help?
2 Why did King tear the red shoe to pieces?
3 What did Benjamin offer to Pete Cameron for helping to smash King's deal?
4 What was strange about the break-ins at the radio parts stores?
5 Why did King want to send Pete Cameron to Boston?
6 Where were Bobby and Jeff playing?
7 Why was Jeff wearing one of Bobby's sweaters?
8 What did Diane think about the advice Doug gave to Bobby?

Read Chapters 4 and 5. Here are some untrue sentences about them. Change them into true sentences.

1 Doug had no idea that Pete Cameron was in contact with his enemies.
2 Diane and Doug planned together to take over Granger Shoe.
3 Bobby couldn't find Jeff because he was hiding in a tree.
4 Steve Carella enjoyed working on cases which involved children.
5 Doug was eager to help the police by answering Carella's questions.
6 Jeff was terrified when Sy and Eddie took him to the farmhouse.
7 Kathy was pleased when Eddie told her about the kidnapping.
8 Eddie had learned how to build radios at college.

Before you read Chapter 6, can you guess what happens next?

1 Will the kidnappers give Jeff back to his father?
2 Will Sy try to kill Jeff?
3 Will Kathy try to help Jeff escape from Sy and Eddie?
4 Will the kidnappers ask Douglas King to pay the ransom?

Read Chapters 6 to 8. Choose the best question-word for each of these questions, and then answer them.

Why / What / Where / Who

1 . . . did Parker, Hawes and Kronig find?
2 . . . did Doug think the kidnappers would do with Jeff?
3 . . . did Sy tell Doug to do?
4 . . . did Pete talk to about Doug's business plans?
5 . . . didn't Doug phone his bank?
6 . . . were Sy and Eddie when Kathy and Jeff tried to escape?
7 . . . happened to prevent Kathy and Jeff from escaping?

Read Chapters 9 and 10. Who said these things, and to whom? Who or what were they talking about?

1 'I don't even like the kid! Why should I be responsible for him?'
2 'I didn't get it by sitting around watching the world go by!'
3 'You're ready to murder a little boy to get what you want!'
4 'If Doug asks me what I think about all this, I'll tell him that I think you're mad.'
5 'I ought to tear it up.'
6 'We just put a bullet in Jeffry Reynolds' head.'
7 'What's really going on here? Have you got plans of your own?'
8 'I guess I know when I'm beaten.'
9 'You're out and I'm in!'

Before you read the rest of the story, what do you think will happen to Douglas King? Choose some of these ideas.

1 He will *pay / refuse to pay* the ransom.
2 He *will help the police in some way / won't help the police at all.*
3 He will *lose / keep* his *job / money / wife.*

Read Chapters 11 and 12. Are these sentences true (T) or false (F)? Rewrite the false ones with the correct information.

1 The kidnappers didn't mind which car King used.
2 Carella thought Doug was right to refuse to help Reynolds.
3 Liz took Bobby to her home because it was safer there.
4 Doug helped the police by keeping the kidnapper talking for as long as possible.
5 The police were able to trace the kidnapper's phone call.
6 When Sy attacked Kathy, Jeff did nothing to help her.
7 When Eddie came in, Kathy was wearing her coat because it was so cold in the farmhouse.

Read Chapters 13 and 14, and then answer these questions.

1 When the Cadillac left the house, who was in it?
2 How did the kidnappers contact the driver of the Cadillac?
3 While Eddie gave instructions to the driver, what did Sy do?
4 What did Eddie threaten to do if they didn't get the money?
5 Why did the kidnappers' plan go wrong?
6 Who caught Sy?
7 What did Jeff tell the police about the kidnappers?
8 What happened to Sy, Eddie and Kathy in the end?
9 What happened to Doug and Diane?

ACTIVITIES

After Reading

1 **Complete these descriptions with the right names, and then choose the best ending for each sentence.**

Kathy / Pete / Eddie / Diane / Doug / Liz / Sy

1 _____ is brave, works hard and loves his family . . .
2 _____ is a violent criminal . . .
3 _____ doesn't think stealing money is wrong . . .
4 _____ talks about a child's life being more important than success . . .
5 _____ is a thief and a kidnapper . . .
6 _____ loves her family and is kind to everyone . . .
7 _____ is kind and helpful to her friends . . .
8 but gives his friends a chance of freedom.
9 but is hard and cruel, and puts money and success first.
10 but wants to live a better life – if he gets the chance.
11 but cheats her husband with a younger lover.
12 but would never hurt a child and always supports her husband.
13 but leaves her husband at the time when he needs her most.
14 but cheats both in love and in business to get what he wants.

2 **Doug King refused to pay a ransom for somebody else's son, and explained why. What other opinions are there on this question?**

1 How did his wife Diane and his son Bobby feel about it?
2 Did Pete Cameron really care about Jeff Reynolds, or did he have other reasons for wanting King to pay the ransom?
3 What was Liz Bellew's position?

4   What should Charles Reynolds have done about it?

5   Did Steve Carella and Lieutenant Byrnes have the same opinion about King's refusal?

6   What is *your* opinion?

3   **Sy told Kathy that Eddie was just 'a cheap crook, and he'll never change'. But is it ever too late to change? Answer these questions and decide what might happen to Eddie after the end of the story.**

1   What did he do when he was fifteen years old?

2   What kind of person is he?

3   Did he care about what happened to Jeff?

4   Who did he listen to more – Kathy or Sy?

5   Is there any job he could do to earn money honestly?

4   **After Eddie's phone call, Douglas King thinks of a plan. Here he is, explaining his plan to Steve Carella. Choose one suitable word to fill each gap.**

'Okay, Carella, listen. You think I'm _____ because I won't pay the ransom, _____ I've been thinking and this is _____ I'll do. The guy who phoned _____ me to leave the house at _____ o'clock, with the money in a _____ box. I have to take the _____ Cadillac, and drive away from the _____. I'm going to do that. But _____ box will be full of old _____, not five hundred thousand dollars, and _____ won't be alone. You, Carella, will _____ hidden in the back of the _____, lying on the floor. You've got _____ gun, haven't you? Good. I have _____ continue driving until someone meets me _____ instructions. There'll probably only be one _____, and as there's two of us, _____ we can catch him and make _____ talk. Okay? Right, let's go.'

97

5 **Which of these ideas about the story do you agree with (A), and which do you disagree with (D)? Explain why you think this.**

1 Jeff should have told the police about Eddie and Kathy.
2 When someone has been kidnapped, the ransom should always be paid, in order to save the person's life.
3 Death should be the punishment for kidnapping a child.

6 **After Kathy shouted the information about Jeff and Sy over the radio, what did she say to Eddie, and to Jeff? Complete her part of this conversation. (Use as many words as you like.)**

EDDIE: What have you done? Are you crazy?

KATHY: I had to, Eddie. I can't _____.

EDDIE: You threw it away! Our five hundred grand!

KATHY: _____.

EDDIE: But I needed it! I needed it so badly. And what about Sy? What will happen to him now?

KATHY: _____.

EDDIE: Sy's my friend. He wanted us all to be rich. How can you do this to him?

KATHY: _____.

EDDIE: I don't believe you. You're lying!

JEFF: She's right, mister. Sy wanted to kill me, too. Will you take me home now, Kathy? Please take me home!

KATHY: _____.

JEFF: But what if it's Sy who comes? I'm frightened of him!

KATHY: _____.

JEFF: The police! But I want *you* to take me home. Please don't leave me here, Kathy!

KATHY: _____.

JEFF: No, I don't want you to go to prison. You're kind. I like you.

KATHY: _____.

JEFF: Okay, I'll say that. I'll say he was the only one.

KATHY: _____.

JEFF: Yes, I understand. It's okay, Kathy, I'll do it.

EDDIE: Come on, can't you? Stop worrying about the kid. He'll be
okay! What about us? What the hell do we do now?

KATHY: _____.

EDDIE: Well, come on then! Let's move before the cops get here!

JEFF: Goodbye, Kathy! I hope you get to Mexico okay.

7 **Here is the beginning of the report Carella writes when the case is
over. Use the notes below to complete his report.**

A small-time criminal, Sy Barnard, planned to kidnap Bobby King,
the eight-year-old son of Douglas King, a director of the Granger
Shoe company. There was another man working with Barnard,
and also a woman, the mysterious 'Kathy'. By mistake . . .

- kidnappers / Jeffry Reynolds / son chauffeur
- King / pay ransom / Jeff / farmhouse / Sands Spit
- Cadillac / money / until / instructions / if police / kill boy
- King / offer / help / catch / drove / hide back of car
- contact / radio / car telephone / unable trace call
- front of car / took phone / directions little by little
- Exit Sixteen / woman / radio / information / Barnard / Jeff
- place Barnard waiting / car / fired / tyre / windows
- Barnard / woods / King / chased / knocked down / held
- Jeff / safe / farmhouse / home-made radio / signs other people
- Jeff / Barnard / not talk / no other arrests

ABOUT THE AUTHOR

Evan Hunter (who is also known as Ed McBain) was born in New York City in 1926. During World War II he served in the US Navy, and then took a university degree, achieving high honours. A few years of teaching in high schools were followed by a job in a literary agency in New York, and he describes himself at this time as 'fiercely ambitious', doing a full day's work in the agency and spending all his nights and weekends writing. His first success, published under the name Evan Hunter, was *The Blackboard Jungle* (1954) – a tough novel of New York life, about an idealistic teacher in a slum high school. It was later made into a film with Glenn Ford and Sidney Poitier.

Since then he has written more than eighty novels, writing under several names, but most famously as Evan Hunter and Ed McBain. He has also written many screenplays, including the one for Hitchcock's film *The Birds*. As Ed McBain, he is the author of the 87th Precinct stories, which is the longest, the most varied, and possibly the most popular crime series in the world. These stories are about a team of policemen, usually including Detective Steve Carella, and are set in an 'imaginary city' – a radically altered New York. There are more than forty 87th Precinct stories: *King's Ransom* (1959) is one of the earlier ones, and two recent titles are *Nocturne* and *The Big Bad City*.

In 1998 Ed McBain received the Diamond Dagger Award from the British Crime Writers Association. He is the first American writer to win this famous award.

OXFORD BOOKWORMS LIBRARY

Classics • Crime & Mystery • Factfiles • Fantasy & Horror
Human Interest • Playscripts • Thriller & Adventure
True Stories • World Stories

The OXFORD BOOKWORMS LIBRARY provides enjoyable reading in English, with a wide range of classic and modern fiction, non-fiction, and plays. It includes original and adapted texts in seven carefully graded language stages, which take learners from beginner to advanced level. An overview is given on the next pages.

All Stage 1 titles are available as audio recordings, as well as over eighty other titles from Starter to Stage 6. All Starters and many titles at Stages 1 to 4 are specially recommended for younger learners. Every Bookworm is illustrated, and Starters and Factfiles have full-colour illustrations.

The OXFORD BOOKWORMS LIBRARY also offers extensive support. Each book contains an introduction to the story, notes about the author, a glossary, and activities. Additional resources include tests and worksheets, and answers for these and for the activities in the books. There is advice on running a class library, using audio recordings, and the many ways of using Oxford Bookworms in reading programmes. Resource materials are available on the website <www.oup.com/elt/bookworms>.

The *Oxford Bookworms Collection* is a series for advanced learners. It consists of volumes of short stories by well-known authors, both classic and modern. Texts are not abridged or adapted in any way, but carefully selected to be accessible to the advanced student.

You can find details and a full list of titles in the *Oxford Bookworms Library Catalogue* and *Oxford English Language Teaching Catalogues*, and on the website <www.oup.com/elt/bookworms>.

THE OXFORD BOOKWORMS LIBRARY
GRADING AND SAMPLE EXTRACTS

STARTER • 250 HEADWORDS

present simple – present continuous – imperative –
can/cannot, must – *going to* (future) – simple gerunds ...

Her phone is ringing – but where is it?

Sally gets out of bed and looks in her bag. No phone. She looks under the bed. No phone. Then she looks behind the door. There is her phone. Sally picks up her phone and answers it. ***Sally's Phone***

STAGE 1 • 400 HEADWORDS

... past simple – coordination with *and*, *but*, *or* –
subordination with *before*, *after*, *when*, *because*, *so* ...

I knew him in Persia. He was a famous builder and I worked with him there. For a time I was his friend, but not for long. When he came to Paris, I came after him – I wanted to watch him. He was a very clever, very dangerous man. ***The Phantom of the Opera***

STAGE 2 • 700 HEADWORDS

... present perfect – *will* (future) – *(don't) have to, must not, could* –
comparison of adjectives – simple *if* clauses – past continuous –
tag questions – *ask/tell* + infinitive ...

While I was writing these words in my diary, I decided what to do. I must try to escape. I shall try to get down the wall outside. The window is high above the ground, but I have to try. I shall take some of the gold with me – if I escape, perhaps it will be helpful later. ***Dracula***

... should, may – present perfect continuous – *used to* – past perfect –
causative – relative clauses – indirect statements ...

Of course, it was most important that no one should see
Colin, Mary, or Dickon entering the secret garden. So Colin
gave orders to the gardeners that they must all keep away
from that part of the garden in future. ***The Secret Garden***

... past perfect continuous – passive (simple forms) –
would conditional clauses – indirect questions –
relatives with *where/when* – gerunds after prepositions/phrases ...

I was glad. Now Hyde could not show his face to the world
again. If he did, every honest man in London would be proud
to report him to the police. ***Dr Jekyll and Mr Hyde***

... future continuous – future perfect –
passive (modals, continuous forms) –
would have conditional clauses – modals + perfect infinitive ...

If he had spoken Estella's name, I would have hit him. I was so
angry with him, and so depressed about my future, that I could
not eat the breakfast. Instead I went straight to the old house.
Great Expectations

... passive (infinitives, gerunds) – advanced modal meanings –
clauses of concession, condition

When I stepped up to the piano, I was confident. It was as if I
knew that the prodigy side of me really did exist. And when I
started to play, I was so caught up in how lovely I looked that
I didn't worry how I would sound. ***The Joy Luck Club***